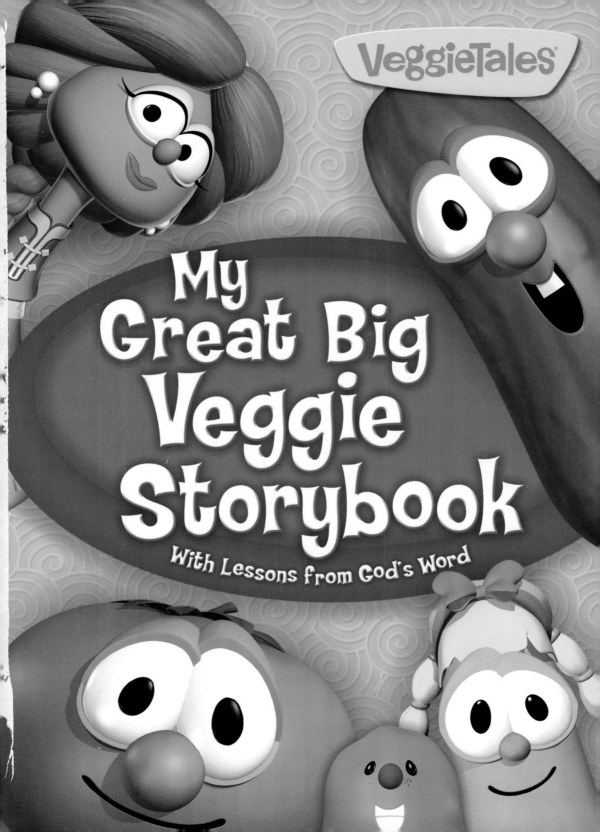

My Great Big Veggie Storybook

With Lessons from God's Word

TM & © 2014 Big Idea Entertainment, LLC. All Rights Reserved.

ISBN 978-1-61795-334-7

Published by Worthy Kids, a division of Worthy Media, Inc.,
134 Franklin Road, Suite 200, Brentwood, Tennessee 37027.

Printed in the U.S.A.

2 3 4 5—LBM—18 17 16 15 14

Table of Contents

God thinks YOU are SUPER and wants you to ...

God thinks YOU are SUPER and wants you to . . .

Make Good Choices

THE GOOD, THE BAD, AND THE SILLY

Bong! The clock struck high noon.

Cowboy Larry was shakin' in his boots—it was the day of his big cattle-drive test at Cowboy School.

Sheriff Bob, the cattle-drive teacher, glanced at the names on his clipboard. "Next up: Cowboy Larry, Botch Scallion, and the Sunburn Kid," he said. Cowboy Larry's heart pounded like a hammer. It was his turn!

It was a tough test! Cowboy Larry would need to move 40 cows from one ranch to another. If he was fast enough, he would pass. If he was a slow-poke, he would fail. And to make things even tougher, this was a team-test. And, Larry's test-taking teammates were none other than those rascals Botch Scallion and the Sunburn Kid.

"Howdy, partners," Cowboy Larry said to Botch and Sunburn.

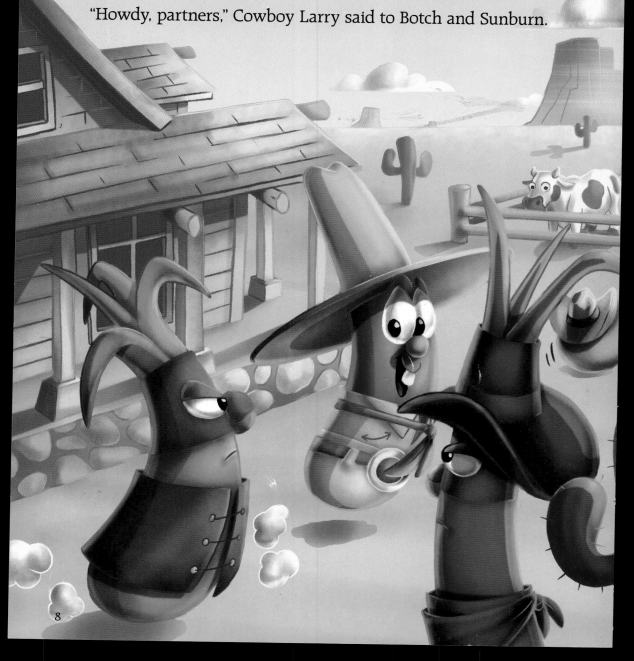

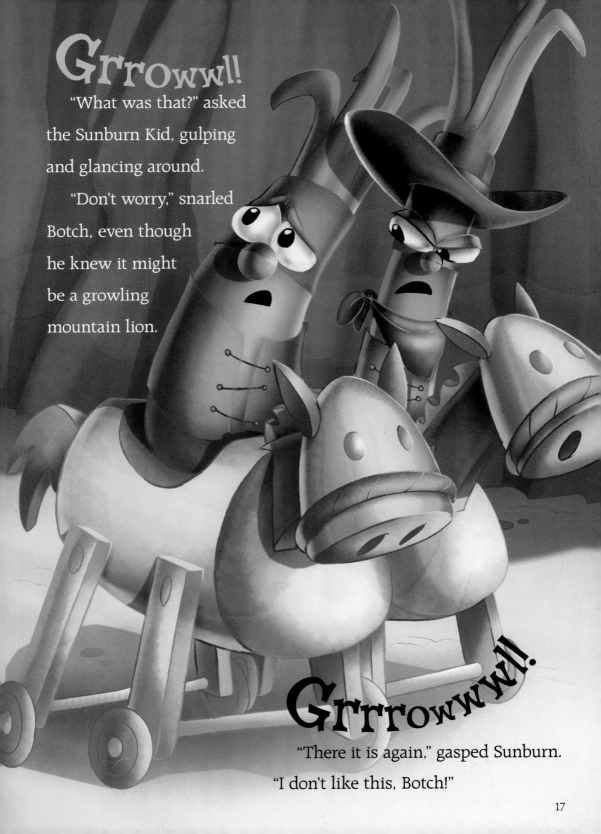

Grrowwl!

"What was that?" asked the Sunburn Kid, gulping and glancing around.

"Don't worry," snarled Botch, even though he knew it might be a growling mountain lion.

Grrrowww!!

"There it is again," gasped Sunburn.
"I don't like this, Botch!"

17

By this time, Cowboy Larry knew he had made the wrong choice. But he also realized that it wasn't too late to change his mind.

It's never too late to do the good thing.

"You asked who's going to know if we cheat," Cowboy Larry said to Botch. "Well . . . I'll know. And so will God. So I'm turning around. Are you coming with me or not?"

"Good riddance," grumbled Botch. *"Adiós, amigo."* But as Cowboy Larry rode out of Dodge Ball Canyon, Botch and the Sunburn Kid suddenly heard it again.

Grrrrrowwwwwl!

Botch rolled his eyes. "That isn't a mountain lion growling," he said to Sunburn. "That's your **stomach** growling."

"Gee, I think you're right," said Sunburn. "I knew I should've ordered *three* flapjack breakfasts this morning at Clint's Covered Wagon Café."

Grrrrrrrowwwwwwwll!

Cows are not especially smart. The more they heard Sunburn's stomach growling, the more afraid they became. They were sure it was the sound of growling mountain lions.

Finally, one of the cows couldn't take it any longer. Terrified, she ran! And when one cow bolted, all of them did.

"*Stampede!*" shouted Botch.

The cattle thundered across the land, kicking up dust. They shook the ground like an earthquake. The result?

"Avalanche!" exclaimed the Sunburn Kid.

Thousands of dodge balls came crashing down from the hills, burying the cowboys in bouncy rubber balls.

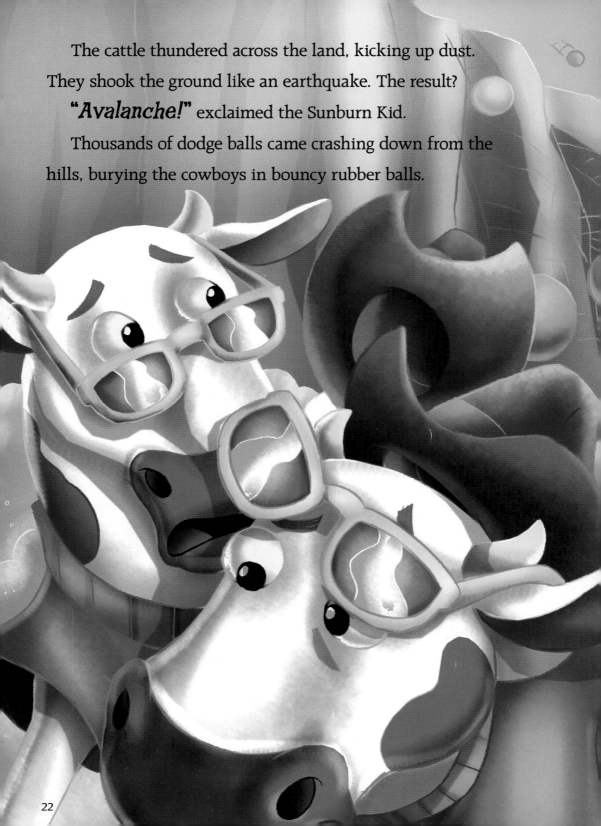

Cowboy Larry got out of the canyon just before the
avalanche. When the dust settled, he was able to gallop
back and throw a rope to Botch and Sunburn.
He pulled them out of the dodge balls,
and he got the cows out, too.

Hip, hip, hooray!! Cowboy Larry had saved the day!

"Good thing I didn't stay with you guys," he told Botch and Sunburn. Cowboy Larry had learned to follow God, rather than follow the crowd—or the herd.

It was dark by the time they returned to the Okie-Dokie Corral.
Miss Kitty, the Cowboy School owner, handed root beers to the
tired cowboys.

"I'm sorry," said Sheriff Bob. "I can't give you your Cattle-Drive
License today."

Cowboy Larry was as happy as could be. Although he didn't
pass the cattle-drive test, he had passed a more important test.
He didn't cheat.

Cowboy Larry had made the **good** choice after all.

The Sunburn Kid, meanwhile, didn't mind that they had failed. Night had fallen in the Wild, Wild West, and he was too busy smearing "moonscreen" on his face.

Splurt!

"Oops—sorry!" he said to Cowboy Larry.

Do not follow the crowd when they do what is wrong.
Exodus 23:2

THINK ABOUT THIS...

When your friends misbehave, do you tell them to stop, or do you go along with the crowd? Usually, it's much easier to go along with the crowd—or to say nothing at all—but that's the wrong thing to do. It's better to stand up for what you know is right.

God's world is a wonderful place, but people who misbehave can spoil things in a hurry. So if your friends behave poorly, don't copy them! Instead, do the right thing. You'll be **super** glad you did . . . and so will God!

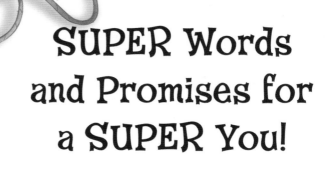

SUPER Words and Promises for a SUPER You!

Our God is a God of second chances!

It's never too late to take the right path.

You never have to be afraid to do what's right

Questions to Talk about with Your SUPER Mom and Dad

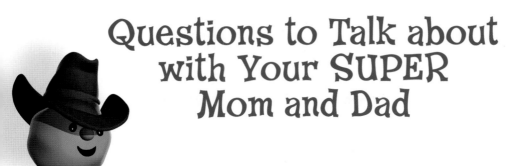

What are some choices you make every day?

How can you help your friends make better choices?

A Prayer

Dear God, help me to make

super choices every day.

Amen

THE KID CRAYON CAPER

Ladies and gentlemen, the story you are about to read is silly. The names have been changed to protect the serious.

Bob and I were celebrating. We had just solved the Case of the Fuzzy Shoestring. It turned out the shoestring wasn't a shoestring after all but a really, really long and fuzzy caterpillar. I named him Harold.

Solving mysteries about caterpillars is part
of my job. I'm a detective. Larry the Cucumber
is my name. My partner is Bob the Tomato.
He carries a badge. I carry a badger.
Don't ask why.

35

When the call came in, Bob answered.

The caller yelled, "Help! Help! Someone *sabotaged* my art show last night!"

"Sabotage!" I cried. "That's when someone secretly ruins somebody else's plans!"

"Don't worry, Kid Crayon, we're on it," Bob said into the phone.

I couldn't believe it. Kid Crayon? We were going to meet the one and only Kid Crayon? **WOW!**

9:27 a.m. I hopped into the car and headed for Madame Blueberry's Gallery of Trendy Art at the corner of Sculpture Street and Painting Place.

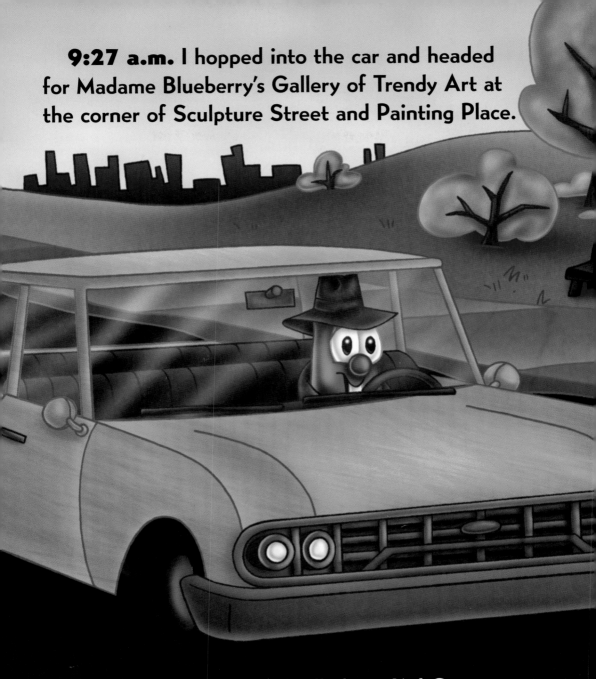

On the way, I told Bob all about Kid Crayon. "He's the most famous crayon artist in the world! Why, his picture of *Mona Sneeza* is worth millions!

I then realized that something was missing, but I couldn't put my finger on it. Bob was being really quiet. "Bob, what's missing?" I asked, turning to look at him.

That was it! *Bob* was missing! Oops. I spun the car around to go get him.

9:46 a.m. Bob and I arrived at the gallery. I parked the car. All I could think about was meeting Kid Crayon. "Are you ready?" I asked Bob.

"Yeah," Bob said as he got out of the car. Then he

Once inside the gallery, Bob got down to business.
"You say the art show was *sabotaged* last night?"
"That's when someone secretly ruins somebody
else's plans," I added to impress Kid Crayon.
He had no idea what I was talking about.

"All I know is that the show was a disaster!"
Madame Blueberry wailed.
    "Just the facts, ma'am," said Bob.

"My employees disappeared," explained Kid Crayon.
"Nobody was there to greet the guests. The food
didn't get served. The lemonade didn't get poured.
And the review in today's *Veggie Gazette* said I'm a
terrible host!"

Kid Crayon was almost in tears. "Who would do this to me? I'm an artistic genius! This could ruin my crayon career! Then what would I do?"

"You could always use felt pens," I suggested.

"Don't worry, Kid Crayon," said Bob.
"Detective Larry and I will get to the bottom
of this—unless he forgets me again."

I didn't hear what Bob said. I was busy
asking Kid Crayon for his autograph.

Off we went. The first employee was Mr. Lunt.
We decided to question him, hoping he might give
us a clue as to what happened at the show.

10:17 a.m. We arrived at the Lunt house. "Someone *sabotaged* Kid Crayon's art show last night," Bob told Mr. Lunt.

"That's when someone secretly ruins somebody else's plans!" I explained helpfully. "Also, you've been reported missing," I said. Of course, that was kind of silly. He was standing right in front of us.

"You worked for Kid Crayon, is that correct?"
I asked Mr. Lunt.

"Yes," he said. "I was Director of Saying Hello to Guests at the Door When They Come In. But I wasn't kidnapped. I quit yesterday—for professional reasons."

"Such as?" Bob asked Mr. Lunt.
Mr. Lunt didn't answer.
He was holding something back, I could tell.
I am a detective, after all. But what wasn't he saying?
I didn't know. He wasn't saying it.

10:29 a.m. We left the Lunt house without any helpful information. It was time to check out the address of the next missing employee: Pa Grape.

To our surprise, he wasn't missing, either. He was right at home cooking a batch of Argentinean cookies with popcorn sprinkles. "I was Kid Crayon's Master Chef in Charge of Making Yummy Stuff to Eat," he told us. "But I quit yesterday—for personal reasons."

10:35 a.m. Pa Grape wouldn't say anymore, so we hurried to the address of the last missing employee on our list: Laura Carrot. She wasn't missing, either. She was home, polishing her collection of metal flamingo statues.

She told us, "I was Kid Crayon's Official Server Who Walks Around and Offers Fizzy Drinks with Little Umbrellas in Them to the Guests. But . . ."

"... I couldn't stand it anymore!" Laura suddenly cried. "None of us could! Kid Crayon used to be a nice guy, but now that he's famous, he thinks he's better than we are!"

"You mean that his ego is out of control?" Bob asked.

"Yes," said Laura. "He was very rude, so we all quit."

I was shocked. Kid Crayon, genius artist, had an ego? **NO!**

Laura added, "He started to treat us like we weren't even there."

Bob mumbled to himself, "Gee, I know how that feels." I couldn't make out what Bob said, but I figured it wasn't important.

There was only one thing to do—confront Kid Crayon.

11:52 a.m. We returned to Madame Blueberry's Gallery of Trendy Art along with Kid Crayon's three not-missing-after-all employees.

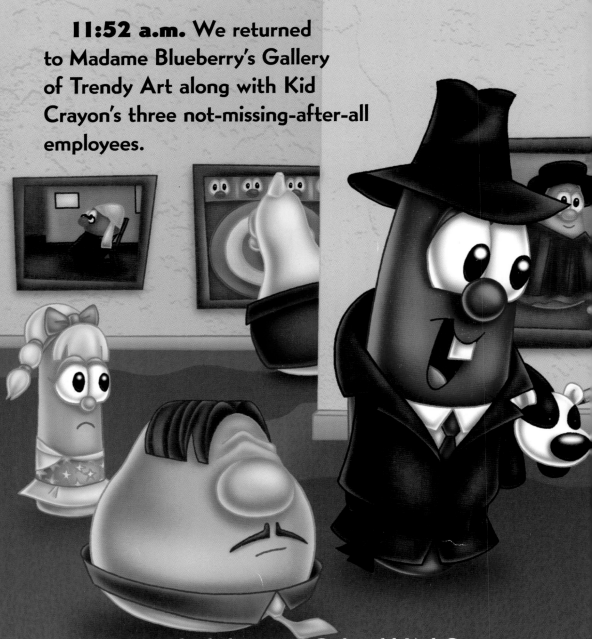

"We've cracked the case," Bob told Kid Crayon. "Turns out that nobody *sabotaged* your art show."

"That's when someone secretly ruins somebody else's plans!" I blurted. I couldn't help it. It was a habit now.

"Seems you let fame go to your head, Kid," Bob went on. "Your employees quit last night. They claim you were *rude* to them. Is this true?"

Kid Crayon looked confused. "I was . . . rude to them?" he asked in shock.

Laura Carrot, Pa Grape, and Mr. Lunt all nodded sadly.

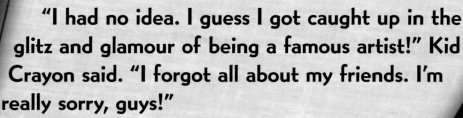

"I had no idea. I guess I got caught up in the glitz and glamour of being a famous artist!" Kid Crayon said. "I forgot all about my friends. I'm really sorry, guys!"

"We forgive you," chorused his three employees. They were so glad to have the old Kid Crayon back!

"Well, that was easy," I said, feeling very good about things. "Another case solved, right partner?" Bob didn't say a word. He was acting really strange. I had never seen him act like this before.

Finally, I just couldn't take it anymore. "Are you OK, Bob?" I asked.

Bob just looked at me. Then he clued me in. "When you ran off without me this morning, it really hurt my feelings. And you didn't even seem to notice that I was sad."

"Wow, I guess I didn't notice. I'm really sorry, Bob," I told him.

I know that it hurts when people forget about you. I never meant to hurt Bob's feelings.

Bob smiled. "You're forgiven, partner!"

. . . The person I value is not proud.
He is sorry for the wrong things
he has done . . .

Isaiah 66:2

THINK ABOUT THIS...

Even if you're a very good person, you're bound to make a mistake or two—everybody does. When you make a mistake or hurt someone's feelings, what should you do? You should say you're sorry and ask for forgiveness. And you should do so sooner, not later.

The longer you wait to apologize, the harder it is on you. So if you've done something wrong, don't be afraid to ask for forgiveness, and don't be afraid to ask for it NOW!

SUPER Words and Promises for a SUPER You!

We need to forgive others because God always forgives us!

Our God is a God of second chances!

The sooner you admit your mistake, the better.

Questions to Talk about with Your SUPER Mom and Dad

Why is it so hard to say you are sorry?

When you say you're sorry, how does that make you feel?

A Prayer

Dear God, when I make a mistake, help me be brave and say I am sorry.
Amen

God thinks YOU are SUPER and wants you to . . .

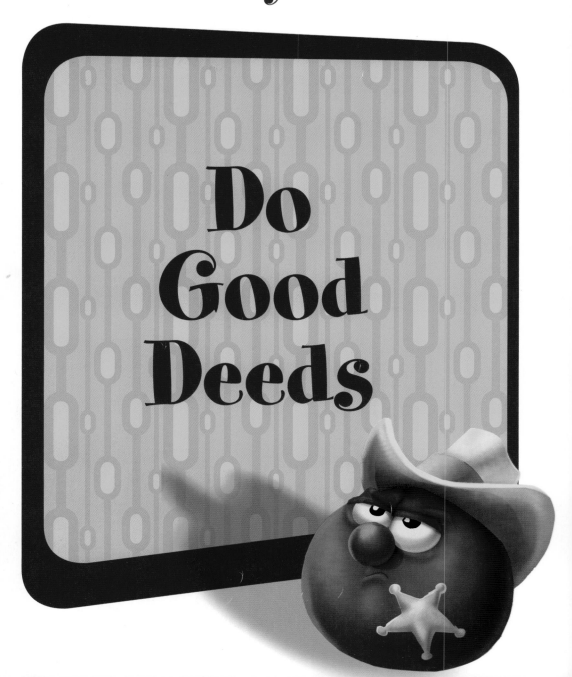

Do Good Deeds

"Grrrrrr

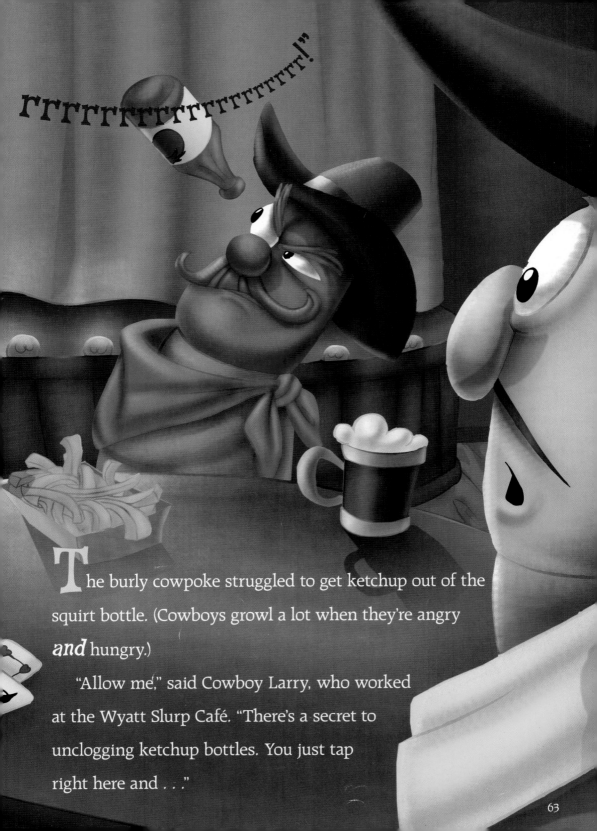

rrrrrrrrrrrrrrrrrrrrrrr!"

The burly cowpoke struggled to get ketchup out of the squirt bottle. (Cowboys growl a lot when they're angry **and** hungry.)

"Allow me," said Cowboy Larry, who worked at the Wyatt Slurp Café. "There's a secret to unclogging ketchup bottles. You just tap right here and . . ."

Squirt!

"Oops," said Cowboy Larry.

"Grrrrrrrrrrrrrr!"

(Cowboys growl even more when they're hungry, angry, *and* covered in ketchup.)

Everyone at the table jumped up so fast that their chairs fell over.

"Grrrrrrrrrrrrrrrrrrrrrrrrrrr!"

"Was that a laugh or a growl?" Cowboy Larry asked, backing up faster than a horse in a snake pit. "Sometimes it's hard to tell."

"Grrrrrrrrrrrrrrrrrrrrrrrr!"

The cowboys forced Cowboy Larry into a corner.

"That's definitely a growl," said Cowboy Larry, grabbing another ketchup bottle. "But I really didn't mean to squirt you. I was just showing that if you tap it here . . ."

Cowboy Larry did it again. He shot another stream of ketchup, splattering a second cowboy.

"Make that double oops," Cowboy Larry said, looking for an escape. Now, there were three loaded ketchup bottles pointed at the trembling cucumber. They moved in closer and . . .

Whap! Whap! Whap!

Three dodge balls zipped across the room. With perfect aim, the balls knocked the ketchup containers cleanly out of the grasp of the angry cowboys.

All eyes turned toward the swinging doors of the restaurant. Standing there was none other than the heroic Sheriff Bob the Tomato—the **Second** Fastest Dodge Ball in the West. He had saved the day!

The cowboys took five angry hops toward the lawman. They locked eyes. The tension in the room was thicker than flies around a skunk's sock drawer . . .

Suddenly Sheriff Bob said with a smile, "You know, if you want to get those ketchup stains out, first you should scrape them with a dull knife and then blot them with a wet sponge."

"Really?" one of the cowboys said.

So, for the rest of the morning, Sheriff Bob and the cowboys shared tips on how to get rid of stains.

He even told the cowboys that he would take their ketchup-covered shirts to the Red River Laundromat to clean them himself.

Sheriff Bob was always doing good deeds like that. He knew that doing good deeds helps make good friends. And he had just made good friends with these boys.

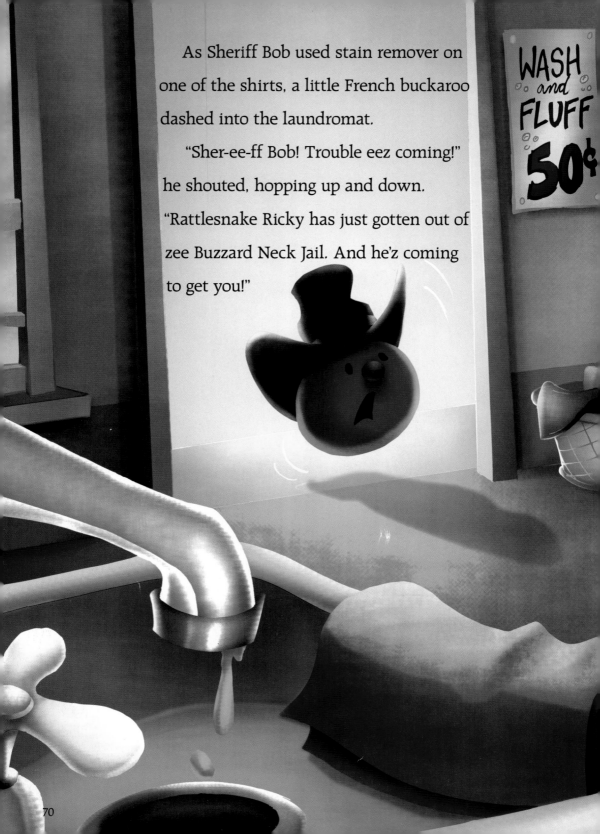

As Sheriff Bob used stain remover on one of the shirts, a little French buckaroo dashed into the laundromat.

"Sher-ee-ff Bob! Trouble eez coming!" he shouted, hopping up and down. "Rattlesnake Ricky has just gotten out of zee Buzzard Neck Jail. And he'z coming to get you!"

WASH and FLUFF 50¢

Sheriff Bob thought back.

He was the one who put Rattlesnake Ricky in

jail for rustling grocery carts.

Rattlesnake Ricky was probably on his way

seeking his revenge. He also happened to be

The Fastest Dodge Ball in the West.

"I can call you a taxi if you need to get out of town," said Cowboy Larry.

"I'm *not* gonna run from Ricky," Sheriff Bob said bravely. "I'm sheriff, and I've got a lot of good deeds to do today."

And that's exactly what Sheriff Bob did.

He helped Mayor Nezzer mow his tumbleweeds.

He helped Miss Kitty get her Buffalo Chips out of the vending machine.

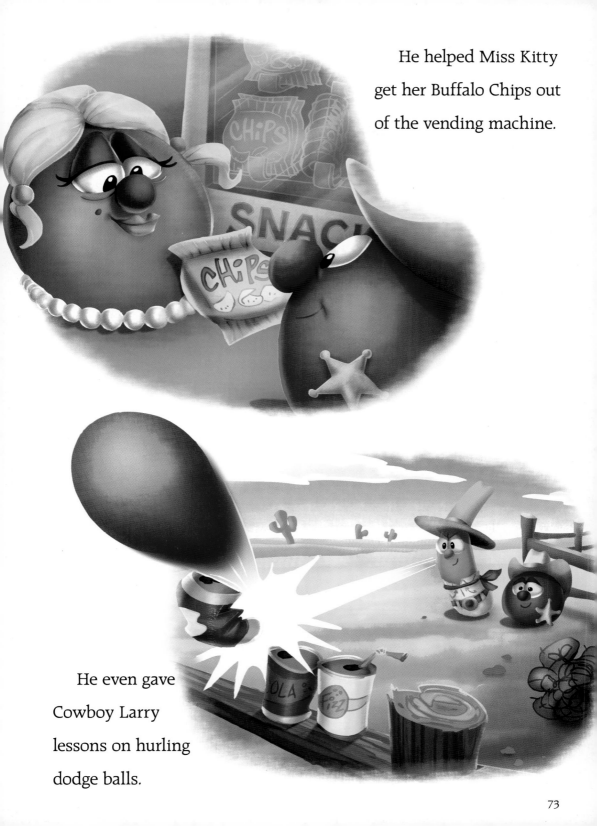

He even gave Cowboy Larry lessons on hurling dodge balls.

Then later that afternoon, a cloud
of dust was spotted on the horizon.
"Zee horse! Zee horse!" shouted the
little buckaroo. "Rattlesnake Ricky eez here!"

74

Frightened women
hurried children into
buildings. Scared cowboys
ran for cover. Only Sheriff
Bob and Cowboy Larry
stood their ground.

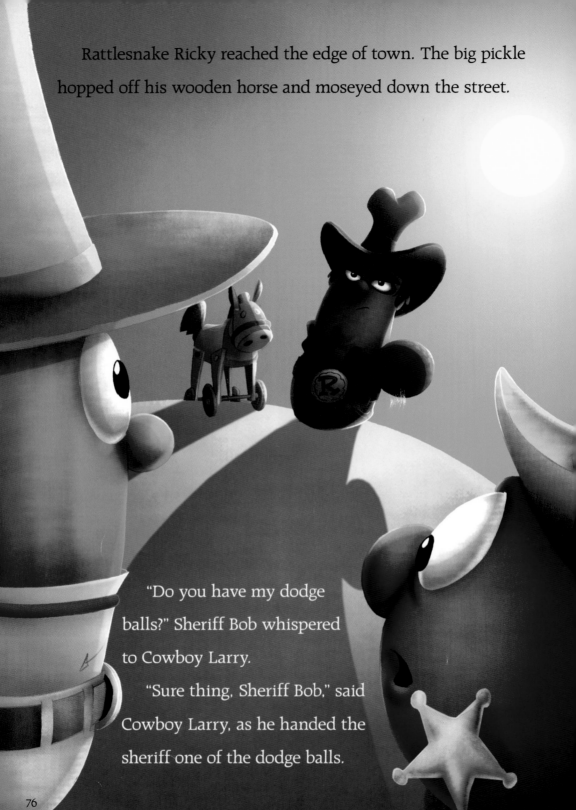

Rattlesnake Ricky reached the edge of town. The big pickle hopped off his wooden horse and moseyed down the street.

"Do you have my dodge balls?" Sheriff Bob whispered to Cowboy Larry.

"Sure thing, Sheriff Bob," said Cowboy Larry, as he handed the sheriff one of the dodge balls.

The sheriff stared at the ball in shock. "It's *flat*," he said.

"That's right," whispered Cowboy Larry. "I learned something important today. Never throw dodge balls at a cactus for target practice."

Cowboy Larry handed Sheriff Bob four more dodge balls. All of them were as flat as a 10-gallon hat under a water buffalo. Cowboy Larry was really starting to worry about what might happen to Sheriff Bob.

"Sheriff Bob, I've been lookin' for ya," snarled Rattlesnake Ricky.

Without a dodge ball, Sheriff Bob was in big trouble.

(Was this the end of Sheriff Bob? Were his days of doing good deeds over? Would Rattlesnake Ricky run Sheriff Bob out of town for good? **Will these questions ever end?**)

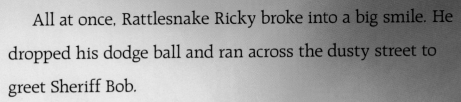

All at once, Rattlesnake Ricky broke into a big smile. He dropped his dodge ball and ran across the dusty street to greet Sheriff Bob.

"I am *SOOOOOOO* happy to see ya, pardner!" said Ricky with a laugh.

Cowboy Larry was puzzled. "Don't you want to get back at Sheriff Bob for putting you in jail?" he asked.

"Of course not!" Ricky exclaimed. "Sheriff Bob was the only person who visited me in jail! He brought me cakes and cookies, and he even read some stories to me!"

Sheriff Bob was only the Second Fastest Dodge Ball in the West. But he was definitely the Fastest *Good Deed Doer.* And this time doing good deeds had made him a good friend.

"From now on, I'm gonna do nothing but good deeds!" Ricky said. "And it's all thanks to my friend Sheriff Bob."

For his first good deed, Rattlesnake Ricky treated Sheriff Bob and Cowboy Larry to some big, juicy burgers at the Wyatt Slurp Café. It was a beautiful end to a glorious day.

"Now, if I can only get the ketchup out of this bottle for my fries," growled Rattlesnake Ricky.

Let us consider how we can stir up
one another to love.
Let us help one another to do good works.
Hebrews 10:24

THINK ABOUT THIS...

An attitude of kindness starts in your heart and works its way out from there. Do you listen to your heart when it tells you to do a good deed? Hopefully, you do. After all, lots of people in the world aren't as fortunate as you are—and some of those folks are living very near you.

So, if you're wondering how to make the world a better place, here's a great place to start: let the Golden Rule be your rule, too: Treat other people like you'd want to be treated if you were in their place.

SUPER Words and Promises for a SUPER You!

True love means thinking of others first

A good deed makes YOU feel GOOD!

Loving means lending a hand.

Questions to Talk about with Your SUPER Mom and Dad

What are some good deeds you can do around your house?

How do you feel when you do a good deed?

A Prayer

Dear Lord, let me be helpful and kind to everybody. And, let me find ways to do good deeds whenever I can.

Amen

God thinks YOU are SUPER and wants you to . . .

Be
Patient

It all started one cold, cold morning. A Viking ship sailed up
to everyone's favorite fast-food place—Barbarian Burger.

"Welcome to Barbarian Burger. May I take your order?"
said the voice over the sail-through speaker.

"Uh . . . we'll take 15 Barbarian Burgers," said Olaf.

So far, so good. In fact, everything was just fine *until* . . .

Everyone in the boat started yelling at
the same time.

"Get me a Big Muck Sandwich with extra seaweed and sod!"
shouted Sven.

"And I'll have the Warrior Meal with Finland fries!" yelled Harold.

"And I want a Slightly Irritated Meal with the Bobble-head
Barbarian Burger toy!" boomed Erik.

"One at a time!" Olaf shouted.

But "one at a time" quickly became "five at a time." No one would wait his turn, and everyone started pushing and arguing. Things couldn't get any worse *until* . . .

Suddenly, another ship rammed right into the side of the Viking boat, almost knocking everyone flat on their faces. The other ship was being steered by the famous Cheese-Packers, a group of wild gourds from Wisconsin. They were delivering "gourda" cheese to Finland.

As everyone struggled to their feet, the Head Cheese asked, "Mind if we cut in line?"

CRASH!

"We were here first!" declared Olaf.

"Too bad!" the Cheese-Packers shouted.

The Cheese-Packers swarmed onto the Viking ship. Then they
all started pushing and shoving, trying to order their food first. Just
when things couldn't get any worse . . .

. . . a huge Wisconsin gourd leaped onto the Viking boat and

smashed right through the bottom of the ship.

"Oops," said the gourd.

Loaded with Vikings and Cheese-Packers, the ship began to sink.

"Quick! Everyone onto the Cheese-Packer ship!" Olaf shouted to

his men. So everyone leaped onto the Cheese-Packer ship—including

the huge gourd.

"Oops," said the gourd.

As the Cheese-Packer ship also began to sink, the Vikings and Cheese-Packers swam to shore.

Then all of them tried to squeeze through the front door of Barbarian Burger at the exact same time. The Vikings and Cheese-Packers smashed open the door and stormed the counter. The teenager at the register just stared in pure terror.

Lyle the Kindly, the smallest Viking of all, hopped onto the counter and spoke up. "Hold it! Hold it!" he cried. The Vikings and Cheese-Packers came to a screeching halt.

"We've got to be patient!" Lyle said. "Being patient means waiting your turn, and it's better than fighting. God tells us that being patient brings peace."

"But does it bring food?" shouted Bjorn.

"We want food! We want food!" the warriors chanted.

Lyle whispered to the guy behind the counter. "How long will it take to get the burgers ready?"

"That's the problem," the worker whispered back. "George the Hamburger Flipper just went home sick."

"We want food! We want food!"

George the Flipper was sick? This was the worst news Lyle could have heard. If he couldn't get these warriors to wait for their meal, they were going to tear the place apart.

"Be patient," Lyle pleaded. Then he whispered again to the worker. "Is there *anything* else you can throw together?"

"Uh . . ." the skinny teenager muttered.   "I . . . uh . . .

can make a pretty good bowl of chicken noodle soup."

"That's it!" exclaimed Lyle. Then he turned back to the Cheese-Packers and Vikings. "George the Hamburger Flipper is home sick. But wait! We're going to get the best chicken noodle soup in the land."

"But what are we supposed to do while we wait?" shouted Erik.

Lyle had to think of something— and fast!

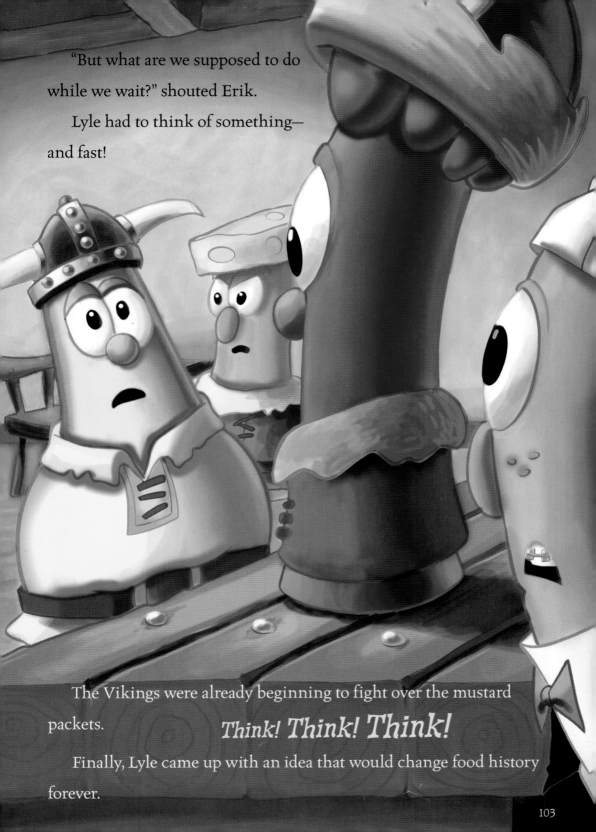

The Vikings were already beginning to fight over the mustard packets. *Think! Think! Think!*

Finally, Lyle came up with an idea that would change food history forever.

"We'll play a game!" Lyle announced. Hopping down from the counter, he grabbed the only chunk of cheese that did not sink with the ship. "I call the game—*food-ball!*"

Making it up on the spot, Lyle told them that the goal of the game was to take turns. "Each team takes turns running with this cheese food-ball," Lyle said. "The Cheese-Packers get four tries to carry the food-ball across a line. The Vikings will try to tackle the Cheese-Packers to stop them from scoring. Then the Vikings get four tries to score. The Cheese-Packers will try to tackle them."

Warriors *love* tackling.

"What do we get if we win?" asked Bjorn.

Lyle hopped back onto the counter and held a golden soup bowl up high. "The winning team gets this!" he declared. "I call it the Chicken Noodle Souper Bowl!"

"OOOOoOOOOOOOOO!" cried both teams.

Lyle marched back and forth like a coach. "Sure, waiting isn't easy," he shouted. "George the Flipper is home sick and the breaks are going against you. But when the waiting gets tough, the tough get waiting! So give it all you've got!

Go out there and play one for the Flipper!"

With a great shout, everyone charged outside onto a frozen field,

where they played the very first food-ball game in history.

The Vikings won the game: 42 to 39. But more important, both teams found out that the game was a lot more fun when the teams took turns with the ball.

In fact, the game wouldn't work at all if the two teams didn't wait their turn.

When the food showed up, a surprising thing happened—even though the Vikings and Cheese-Packers were very hungry.

This time, everyone waited in line for the chicken noodle soup *and* they were all very polite.

"After you," Erik said to the big gourd.

"No, you first," said the gourd with a grin.

Yes, some amazing things happened that day. Olaf, the star of the game, was asked to have his picture on a cereal box.

Sven learned it was fun to do a little dance whenever he scored.

And Ottar led everyone in a very special fight song:

Cheer, cheer! We're glad that you came!
We've got the cheese ball. Let's play the game!
If the other team is late,
That's quite okay 'cause we've learned to wait!

But the most amazing thing of all was that all the wild warriors

learned that being patient was more fun than bickering.

Now *that's* something to cheer about!

It is better to be patient than to fight . . .
Proverbs 16:32

THINK ABOUT THIS...

Patience is a very good thing. But for most of us, patience can also be a very hard thing. After all, there are many things that we want, and we want them NOW!

Are you having trouble being patient? If so, remember that patience takes practice, so keep trying. And if you make a mistake, don't be too upset. After all, if you're going to be a really patient person, you shouldn't just be patient with others; you should also be patient with yourself.

SUPER Words and Promises for a SUPER You!

Being patient shows we care!

God always keeps His promises, even if we have to wait a while.

God's timing is always perfect!

Questions to Talk about with Your SUPER Mom and Dad

When you have to wait for things, they can be even better. How can you be better at waiting for things?

Why is it hard to wait to get what you want?

A Prayer

God, sometimes it's hard to be patient. Help me to be patient and kind, even when it's hard.

Amen

God thinks YOU are SUPER and wants you to . . .

Take Turns

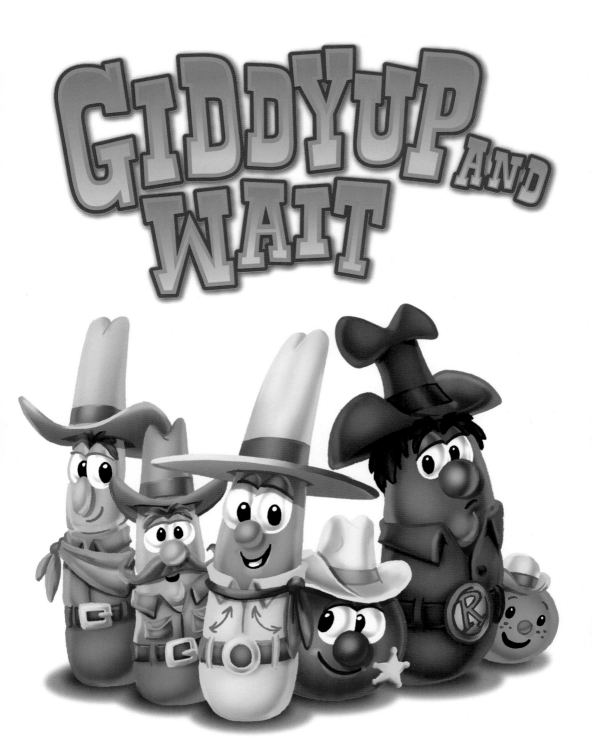

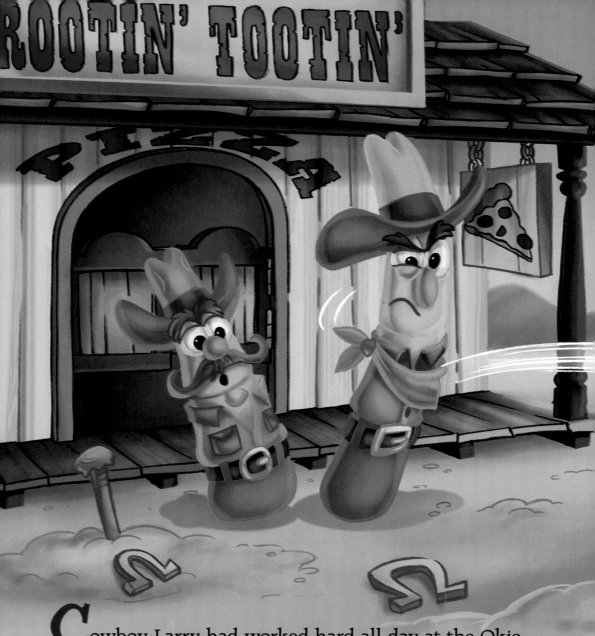

Cowboy Larry had worked hard all day at the Okie Dokie Ranch. He hoped to get out of the hot sun, dust the dirt off, and eat a heap of pizza.

As Larry moseyed up to the Rootin' Tootin' Pizza Place, he saw two cowpokes playing a game of horseshoes outside. It looked liked fun!

Clank! Clank!

The horseshoes made a steely sound as the cowpokes threw them against a metal pole in the middle of a sandpit.

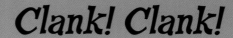

CLANK!

"That looks like more fun than a barrel full of root beer!" Larry said. "Can I please have a try?"

"Sorry, pardner. We're playing best out of 11," one of the cowboys said.

"You can have a turn when we're done," said the other.

"All righty," Cowboy Larry said cheerfully.

Cowboy Larry waited—and **waited**—and **waited** some more. They just kept playing and playing.

Cowboy Larry's turn never came. "Oh, well," Larry shrugged and said. "Guess I'll do something else."

Cowboy Larry went inside the Rootin' Tootin' Pizza
Place. He spotted a video game in the corner. Larry hadn't
played a game of Rodeo Roundup in a long time.

"Oh, boy, I can't wait to play!" exclaimed Larry.

As Cowboy Larry moseyed up to the machine, Philippe the French buckaroo jumped in front of him.

"It eez my turn!" said Philippe.

"All righty," said Larry. He didn't mind waiting. "I'll just take a turn when you're done."

Cowboy Larry waited—and **waited**—and **waited** some more. The wait felt longer than the tail on an old mare. Larry's turn never came.

By this time, Cowboy Larry was feeling a little sad. "I know," he said. "I'll play 'On Top of Ole Meatball' on the jukebox. That song always cheers me up."

Cowboy Larry headed for the jukebox. But Rattlesnake Ricky beat Larry to it and loaded the machine with quarters.

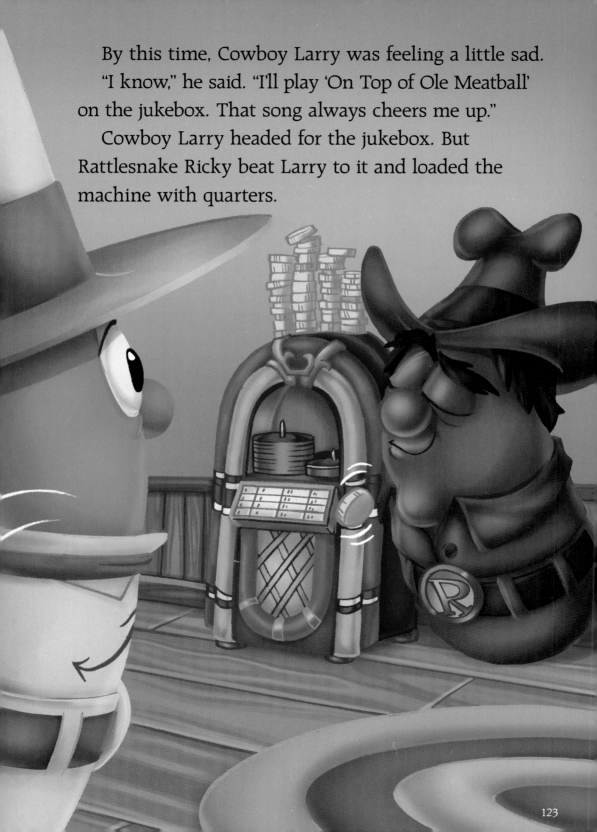

"'Mary Had a Bronkin' Buck' is the best song ever," Rattlesnake Ricky said, as he pushed the buttons on the jukebox. "I can hear it over and over again. That song never gets old."

"All righty," Cowboy Larry said. "I'll just listen to 'On Top of Ole Meatball' when it's my turn."

MARY HAD A BRONKIN' BUCK, BRONKIN' BUCK, BRONKIN' BUCK...

Larry waited—and **waited**—and **waited** some
more. "Mary Had a Bronkin' Buck" played once. It played
twice. It played again—and again—and again . . .
Cowboy Larry's turn never came.

Cowboy Larry was feeling sadder than a pig in a wash tub on a Saturday night. He didn't think he would have any fun that day. That was until Sheriff Bob burst into the pizza place.

"I have big news!" Sheriff Bob announced. "There's a new horse at the Okie Dokie Ranch! She's the finest palomino I've ever seen . . ."

SPPFFUH!

The surprised cowboys spit out their root beer.

"**Yee-ha!**" they cried, and rushed out to the Okie Dokie Ranch to check out the new palomino.

Cowboy Larry followed them. He couldn't wait to take a turn riding the new filly.

They all found the palomino in the Okie Dokie Corral at the Okie Dokie Ranch. Sheriff Bob had told the truth. She was the finest horse they had ever seen.

"I want to ride her first!" the carrot brothers cried at the same time.

"*Me first!* Pleeze!" said Philippe.

"I reckon I'd like to ride her first," said Rattlesnake Ricky.

"I have an idea," said Cowboy Larry.
"We can draw straws from that haystack
over there. Whoever draws the longest
straw can go first. The cowboy with the
second longest straw goes next. We keep
going like that until everyone has a turn."

Philippe was too excited to wait. He jumped right
on the horse! "*Giddyup!*" he yelled. He bounced up
and down on the saddle. Then Philippe lost control. He
bounced off the horse and onto the dirt!

Rattlesnake Ricky didn't wait for Philippe to get back up.
Ricky jumped on the palomino next and galloped off.

While Philippe rolled in the dirt, everybody else watched from the fence.

"It is my turn next!" said one buckaroo.

"No, it's my turn next!" said another.

The cowboys were more excited than two birds at a worm convention. They began pushing each other. Suddenly the two arguing cowboys tumbled over the fence. They landed in a squishy pit of mud.

SPLAT!

Philippe was upset with Rattlesnake Ricky. "It eez steel my turn!" he cried, wiping the mud from his hat.

Then the little pea jumped on the horse and squeezed himself into the saddle with Ricky. As Philippe shoved and pushed, the horse began to **wobble**. Ricky's hat fell over his eyes. He lost control of the palomino.

Philippe and Rattlesnake Ricky tumbled off of the palomino—and right into a trough of messy pig slop! **SPLAT!**

The cowboys were not hurt, but the poor palomino was in more trouble than a coffee bean in a grinder. She rolled out of the corral and out of control. She rolled and rolled—right for the canyon!

"*Oh no!*" shouted Cowboy Larry. He grabbed a rope and hurried after the horse.

Cowboy Larry raced to save the palomino. He lassoed the horse in the nick of time and rode her back into the corral.

The other cowpokes felt bad about how they had acted. The carrot brothers were soaked in mud. Philippe and Ricky were coated in pig slop.

"You were right, Larry," admitted Rattlesnake Ricky. "We should take turns, and do things fair and square."

"Tell us more about zee drawing of zee straws," said Philippe.

"How do these look?" the cowpokes asked, showing their drawings of drinking straws to Larry.

Cowboy Larry smiled and said, "Let me explain again how this works."

After hearing Cowboy Larry's explanation, the cowpokes drew straws from the haystack. Larry didn't get the longest straw. But they were so grateful that Cowboy Larry had saved the palomino, they let him go first.

They all took turns riding the horse
until everyone had a chance to ride.

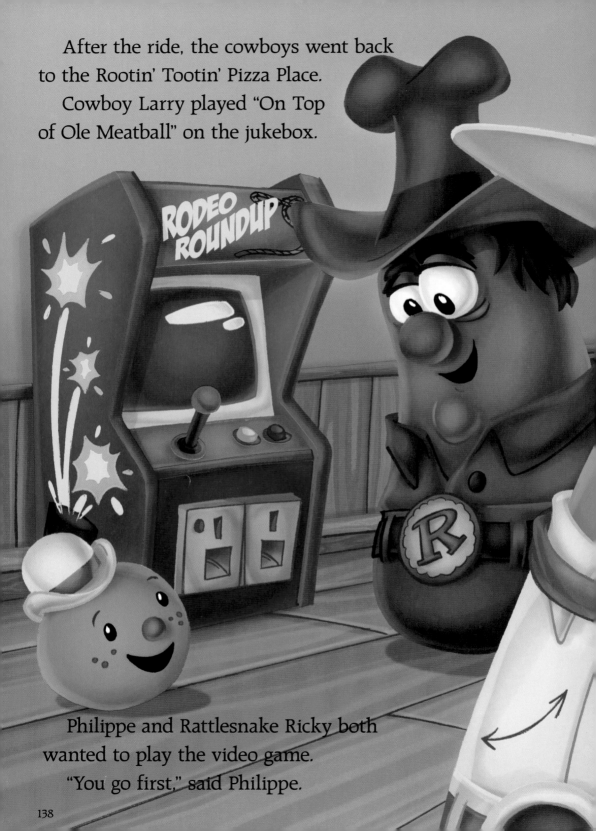

After the ride, the cowboys went back
to the Rootin' Tootin' Pizza Place.
Cowboy Larry played "On Top
of Ole Meatball" on the jukebox.

Philippe and Rattlesnake Ricky both
wanted to play the video game.
"You go first," said Philippe.

"No, you," said Rattlesnake
Ricky.

"No, after you," said Philippe.

"After you. I insist!" said Ricky.

Cowboy Larry grinned. Taking
turns sure made things 'round
here much nicer!

139

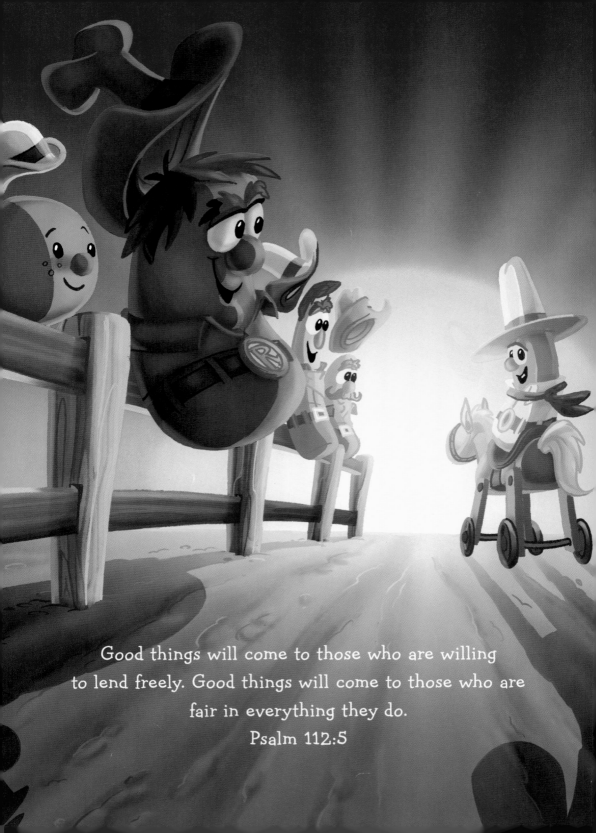

Good things will come to those who are willing
to lend freely. Good things will come to those who are
fair in everything they do.

Psalm 112:5

THINK ABOUT THIS...

When we're standing in line or waiting our turn, it's tempting to scream, "Me first!" It's tempting, but it's the wrong thing to do. We shouldn't push ahead of other people; instead, we should do the right thing—the polite thing—by saying, "You first!"

Sometimes, waiting your turn can be hard, especially if you're excited or in a hurry. But even then, waiting patiently is the right thing to do. Why? Because parents say so, teachers say so, and, most importantly, God says so!

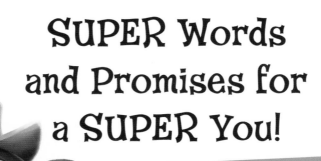

SUPER Words
and Promises for
a SUPER You!

Taking turns makes great friends

We can give because God gave!

Don't just take a turn, GIVE a turn!

Questions to Talk about with Your SUPER Mom and Dad

Has someone ever taken your turn?
How did that make you feel?

Why is it good for you to wait your turn?

A Prayer

God, help me remember
to follow the Golden Rule
and wait my turn. Amen

Ladies and gentlemen,
the story you are about to read is silly.
The names have been changed
to protect the serious.

It was a slow day at police headquarters. Bob
worked on a puzzle, while I read a book: *The Mop
That Ate Cleveland*. The book was about a giant
mop that wiped out an entire city.

It was pretty scary stuff.
But it didn't bother me. After
all, I was a detective.

My name is Detective Larry
the Cucumber, and my partner
is Bob the Tomato. Bob carries
a badge. I carry a badger.
Don't ask why.

12:53 p.m. I was just getting to the scariest part of my book when all of a sudden—

RINNNNNG!

"AHHHHHHHHHHHHHH!"

The phone call startled me, and I nearly jumped out of my skin.

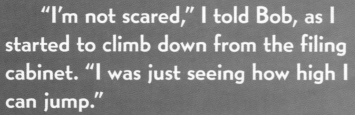

"I'm not scared," I told Bob, as I
started to climb down from the filing
cabinet. "I was just seeing how high I
can jump."

Detectives never know when they
will have to jump.

As it turned out, the phone call was
important.

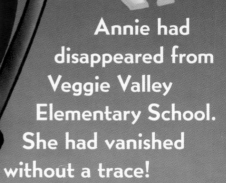

Annie had
disappeared from
Veggie Valley
Elementary School.
She had vanished
without a trace!

149

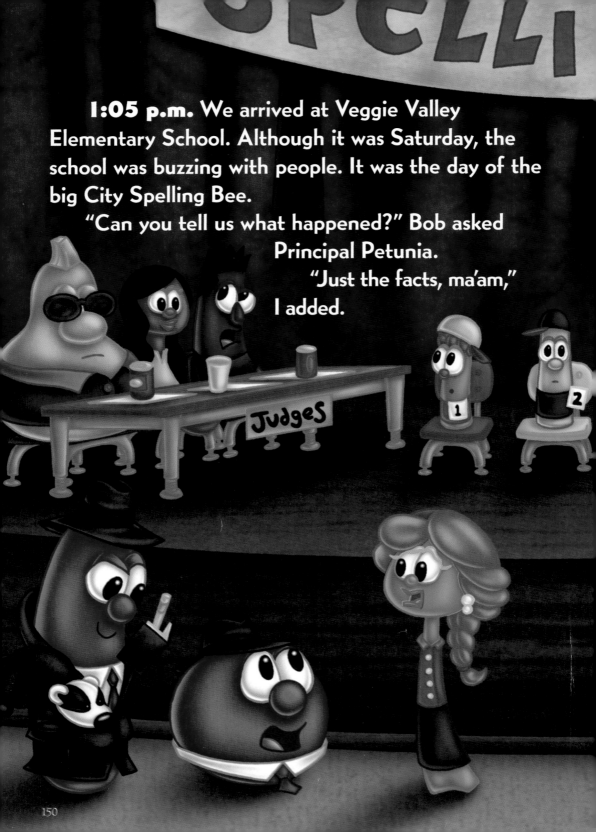

1:05 p.m. We arrived at Veggie Valley Elementary School. Although it was Saturday, the school was buzzing with people. It was the day of the big City Spelling Bee.

"Can you tell us what happened?" Bob asked Principal Petunia.

"Just the facts, ma'am," I added.

Judges

1

2

"And by the way, *facts* is spelled *F-A-X*." In my day, I was quite the speller.

Petunia tried to tell me that the word *facts* was spelled *F-A-C-T-S*. Can you believe it?

Then Petunia went on, "Our spelling bee is supposed to start at two o'clock. Annie is one of the school's best spellers. But she's gone!"

"*Gone.* That's spelled *G-A-W-N*," I said, writing in my notebook. But Petunia tried to tell me that *gone* was spelled *G-O-N-E*.

Can you believe it?

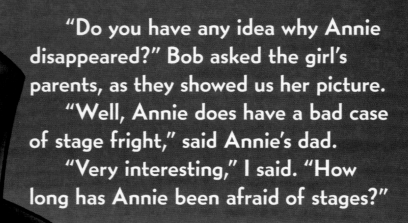

"Do you have any idea why Annie disappeared?" Bob asked the girl's parents, as they showed us her picture.

"Well, Annie does have a bad case of stage fright," said Annie's dad.

"Very interesting," I said. "How long has Annie been afraid of stages?"

"She *isn't* afraid of stages," said Annie's mom. "Stage fright means she's afraid of getting up in front of lots of people—like at this spelling bee."

"Whenever Annie is afraid, she hides," added her dad. "We've tried to teach her that whenever she's afraid, she should talk to God or to us."

"It must be tough being scared," I said. "I'm glad we detectives are never afraid."

Bob just rolled his eyes.

1:15 p.m. Bob searched the first floor of the school, while I checked upstairs. I began by looking inside the first-grade classroom, which was empty. No sign of Annie.

Then I went to the second-grade classroom—still no Annie.

Finally, I peeked inside the third-grade classroom.
That's strange, I thought to myself. The room was very
dark and seemed to be filled with lots of stuff.
　　"It's a good thing we detectives are never afraid,"
I reminded myself as I walked into the spooky room.

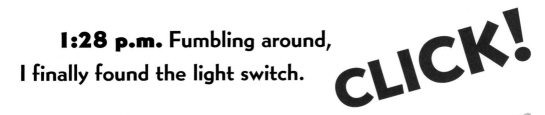

1:28 p.m. Fumbling around,
I finally found the light switch.

CLICK!

"AHHHH!"

I found myself staring at a huge mop.
Was *this* the Mop That Ate Cleveland?
And was *this* mop about to wipe me
off the face of the Earth?

Then it dawned on me. I wasn't inside the third-grade classroom. I was inside the janitor's closet with lots and lots of mops!

"AHHHHHHHHHHHHHH!"

I turned to run but tripped over a bucket and crashed against a rolled-up hose. The hose curled around me like a snake.

With the hose wrapping me up, I yanked the door handle, and . . .

The handle came off! I was trapped in a janitor's closet with the Mop That Ate Cleveland and the Garden Hose of Doom!

I bumbled backward against the wall.

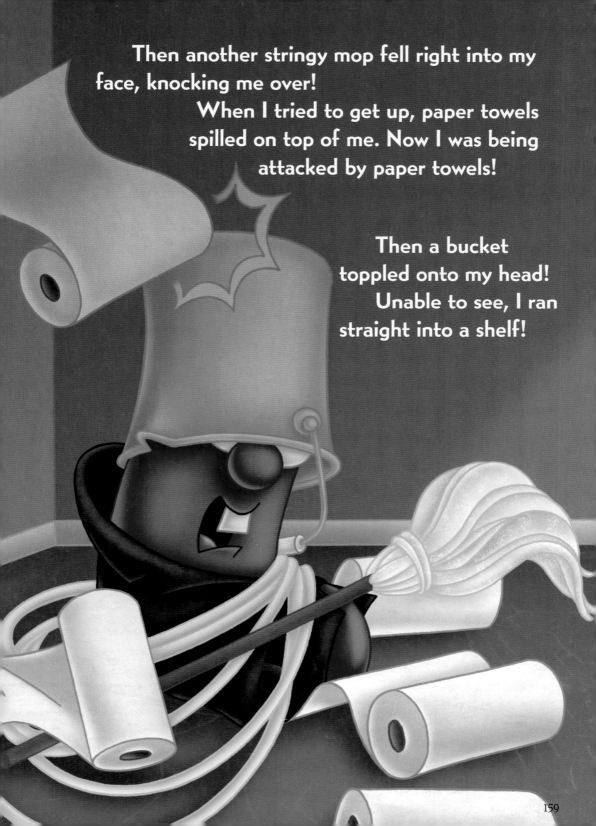

Then another stringy mop fell right into my face, knocking me over!

When I tried to get up, paper towels spilled on top of me. Now I was being attacked by paper towels!

Then a bucket toppled onto my head! Unable to see, I ran straight into a shelf!

159

With the bucket still on my head, I dashed toward the door. I wanted to bust through. I wanted to—

"WHOOOOOOOAAAAA!"

Someone opened the door just as I was about to smash through. Unable to stop, I crashed into the hallway wall and wound up in a crazy heap on the floor.

"Are you all right?" asked a girl, as she lifted the bucket from my head.

I found myself looking right into Annie's face.

1:45 p.m. Bob, Petunia, and Annie's parents rushed over.

"What's all the racket?" asked Bob. "We heard the noise and—*Annie!*"

When everyone spotted Annie, they were shocked and overjoyed.

"Where have you been?" asked her mom.

"I've been praying," Annie said.

"But then I heard a noise coming from the janitor's closet, and that's when I found Detective Larry." From the floor, I gave a weak smile. "Anyone need their floor waxed?"

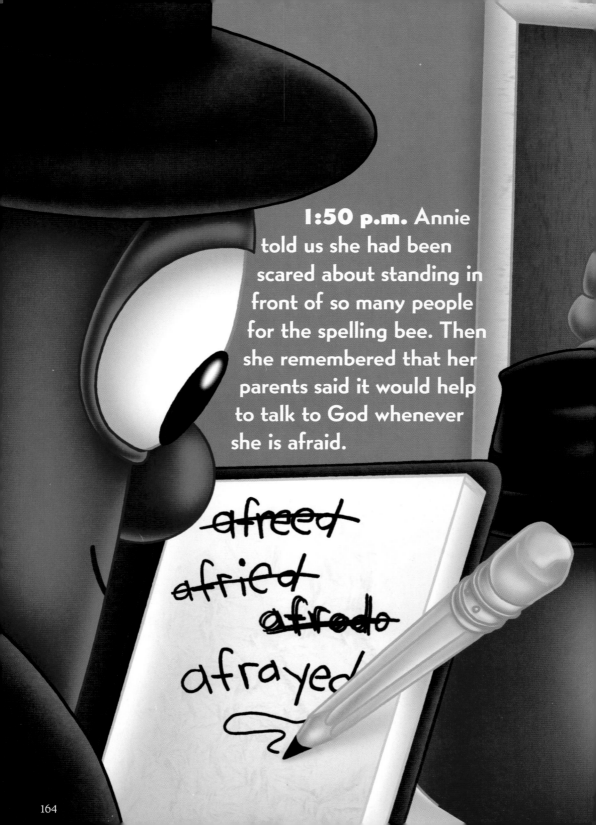

1:50 p.m. Annie told us she had been scared about standing in front of so many people for the spelling bee. Then she remembered that her parents said it would help to talk to God whenever she is afraid.

"So I went into an empty classroom to pray," said Annie. "And you know what? It helped. It *really* helped to tell God about my fears."

I made a note of that. "Afraid is spelled *A-F-R-A-Y-E-D*," I said. But Petunia tried to tell me that *afraid* is spelled *A-F-R-A-I-D*. Can you believe it?

3:00 p.m. The spelling bee was over, and Annie did great. She still had some butterflies in her belly, but she stood in front of the crowd anyway. What a brave girl!

Although Annie didn't win the spelling bee, she came away with the third-place ribbon. In fact, the only thing that went wrong during the entire spelling bee was when Junior Asparagus was asked to spell *mop*.

That's when I ran out of the room screaming.
    But then I remembered. I could talk to God when I am afraid. And that really helped!
    Can you believe it?

THINK ABOUT THIS...

Everyone of us is afraid sometimes. Maybe we are afraid of the dark. Good news! We can always talk to God. God is always ready to hear our prayers, and He can help us be brave when we're afraid.

It's okay to be afraid—all of us are fearful from time to time. And it's good to know that we can talk about our fears with loved ones and with God. When we do, we'll discover that fear lasts for a little while, but love lasts forever.

SUPER Words and Promises for a SUPER You!

God is bigger than the Boogie-Man

When you are afraid sing a happy song and say a prayer.

We don't have to be afraid, because God is always looking out for us!

Questions to Talk about with Your SUPER Mom and Dad

What are things that make you afraid?

Can you say a prayer in your own words to ask God to help you not be afraid?

A Prayer

God, thank You for helping me not be afraid.
Amen

He's slower than a speeding snail—lazier than a drowsy dog—unable to lift dirty clothes from a bedroom floor!

Look! In the hammock—it's a slug! It's a bump on a log! No, it's—*Spud the Dud!*

Yes, it's Spud the Dud.
He's a strange potato who
came to Bumblyburg with powers far less
than those of normal citizens.
It had all started one day when he arrived
at the home of Junior Asparagus . . .

"I don't wanna walk the dog!" Junior whined. "Can't I do it later?"

"But Wonder-Pup is *your* dog," said Junior's mom. "She's your responsibility—your duty. When we got Wonder-Pup, you agreed to walk and feed her."

That was true. But that was then. Now, Junior just thought that Wonder-Pup was a great big bother.

"Junior, it's important to do small jobs when you're young," said Mom Asparagus. "It'll get you ready for big responsibilities when you're older."

Junior moaned as he trudged outside with the dog.

Suddenly Junior heard a voice say, "You're right. That dog *is* a big bother."

"Who said that?" Junior asked, whirling around.

Junior was stunned to see a strange potato in his yard. The potato was lying in a hammock, wearing an old, tattered superhero suit.

Junior asked again, "Who are you?"

"The name is Spud the Dud, and I think you're right," said the potato. "Why walk the dog when you can lie around eating cheesy puffs? How would you like to join me in my quest to rid the world of 'big bother' responsibilities? You'll even get to wear a spiffy superhero sidekick suit." The potato added, "What d'you think?"

"I think I would really like to be a superhero," Junior said. He was thrilled when Spud the Dud gave him his own special superhero sidekick suit to wear!

Little did Junior know that it was all a trick! The moment he put on the sidekick suit, Spud pulled out a remote control. He pointed it at Junior and pushed a button.

CLICK!

The remote controlled Junior's suit. It made him move. But worst of all, it made Junior do everything for Spud the Dud!

"HA-HA-HA-HA!" Spud cackled. (He had been first in his class in sinister laughing.) "Junior, you are in my power! Soon all the children of Bumblyburg will be serving *me!*" Spud clicked the remote and snarled, "Get me more cheesy puffs!"

"Help!" cried Junior in shock.

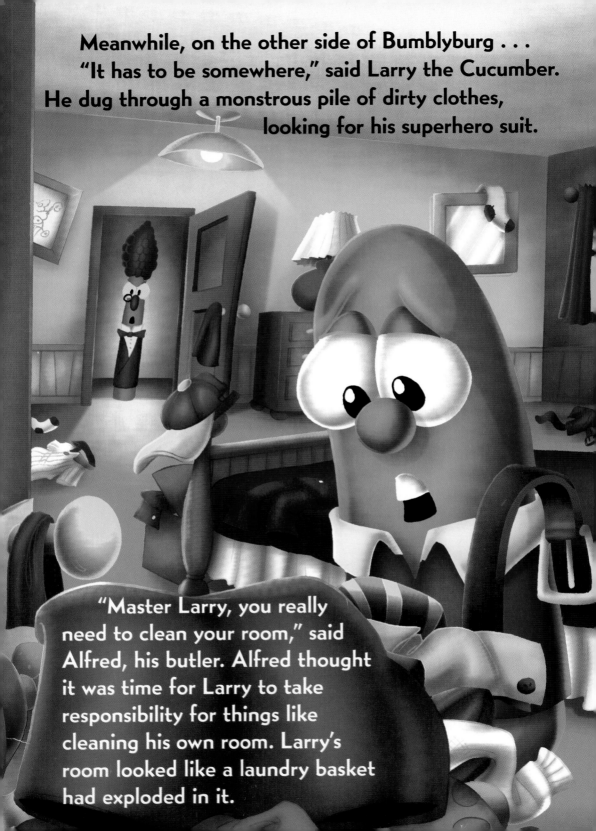

Meanwhile, on the other side of Bumblyburg . . .
"It has to be somewhere," said Larry the Cucumber.
He dug through a monstrous pile of dirty clothes,
looking for his superhero suit.

"Master Larry, you really need to clean your room," said Alfred, his butler. Alfred thought it was time for Larry to take responsibility for things like cleaning his own room. Larry's room looked like a laundry basket had exploded in it.

RINGGGG!

Alfred picked up the phone. It was Mayor Blueberry, and there was big trouble in Bumblyburg.

"Quick, Master Larry!" Alfred said. "Spud the Dud is taking control of the city's children!"

"But I can't find my suit!" Larry shouted. He finally dug up an old, torn superhero suit and said, "I guess this old thing will have to do."

So Larry dashed into his closet and came out as the plunger-headed hero—LarryBoy!

LarryBoy raced to Junior's neighborhood. The superhero couldn't believe his eyes. Spud the Dud was using his remote to control kids. He was making them do chores, scratch his head, and fan him with palm branches.

"Let those kids go free, you stuffed potato!" LarryBoy declared.

"Try to make me, PickleBoy!" scowled the lazy tater.

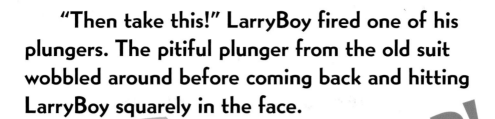

"Then take this!" LarryBoy fired one of his plungers. The pitiful plunger from the old suit wobbled around before coming back and hitting LarryBoy squarely in the face.

THOMP!

"Now I know why I stopped using this old suit," LarryBoy said. But with a plunger stuck on his face, it sounded more like, "Nahow Ino why Istopd singing dis moldy shoot."

185

THONK!

Yanking the plunger loose,
LarryBoy tried again. This time
the plunger shot straight and hit
Spud's hammock squarely.

"It's working!" LarryBoy
shouted, as he fired his second
plunger at the potato.

But the second plunger struck the back of a passing train instead! "It *isn't* working!" cried LarryBoy.

The racing train yanked LarryBoy into the air, dragging him and Spud behind it. As LarryBoy and Spud whipped wildly around the bend, the LarryBoy Cell Phone rang. It was Alfred.

"Make it fast, Alfred!" LarryBoy yelled. "I'm kind of busy being pulled to my doom because my plunger is stuck to a train."

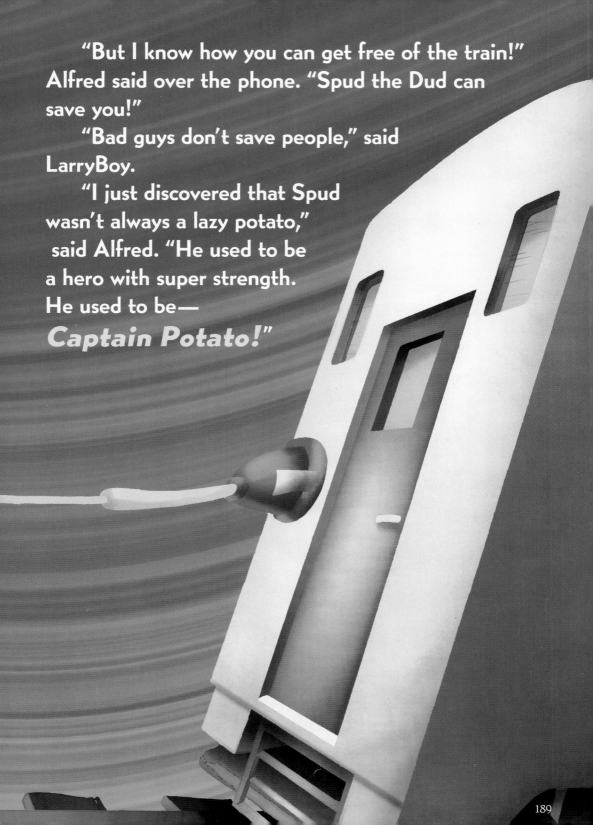

"But I know how you can get free of the train!" Alfred said over the phone. "Spud the Dud can save you!"

"Bad guys don't save people," said LarryBoy.

"I just discovered that Spud wasn't always a lazy potato," said Alfred. "He used to be a hero with super strength. He used to be—

Captain Potato!"

189

LarryBoy couldn't believe his ears. Neither could Spud when LarryBoy tried to tell him that he was once Captain Potato.

"If I'm Captain Potato, then I would have a cape," Spud said. "Where's my cape?"

"Good point," said LarryBoy.

But that's when LarryBoy spotted it. Underneath a big splotch of cheese on Spud's hammock, LarryBoy saw the letters *CP—Captain Potato!*

"Look!" LarryBoy shouted. "Your hammock must have been your cape at one time!"

Spud was shocked, but then it all started to come back to him. Maybe he did have more power than he thought. Yes, deep down, he wasn't always a lazy tater.

With a burst of super energy, Spud pulled his
hammock apart and put on his cape. It's true! He
was Captain Potato! He was stronger than a racing
train! In fact, Captain Potato was so strong that he
brought the train to a screeching stop.

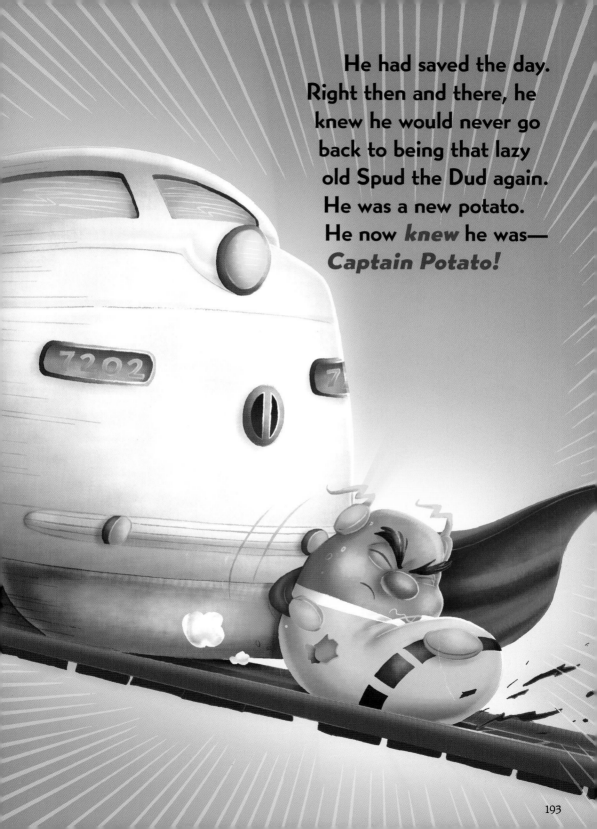

He had saved the day. Right then and there, he knew he would never go back to being that lazy old Spud the Dud again. He was a new potato. He now *knew* he was— *Captain Potato!*

The next morning, while Junior happily walked his dog, he glanced up. Look! Up in the sky—it's a bird! It's a badly dressed burrito! No, it's *Captain Potato!*

Captain Potato had learned that using his super powers was a lot more fun than being lazy. He took all the sidekick suits back and threw them away so that the kids were free again! Junior had learned that being lazy isn't as much fun as it looks and that real happiness comes from being responsible and doing what you're supposed to do, not just what you want to do.

As for LarryBoy—he was right behind Captain Potato, swinging from tree to tree with his plunger ears. "Hey, this old suit works after all!" LarryBoy shouted in delight. "Maybe I can—"

"Oops." After LarryBoy's plunger popped loose, he crashed into a garbage can.

"Maybe I'd better clean up my room after all," LarryBoy muttered from inside the can.

People who refuse to work want things and get nothing. But the longings of people who work hard are completely satisfied.

Proverbs 13:4

THINK ABOUT THIS...

Sometimes it is easy to be lazy. We forget to do our chores. If you're having a little trouble getting something done, don't give up.

When you try hard—and keep trying—you can do amazing things, but if you quit at the first sign of trouble, you'll miss out. Here's a good rule to follow: When you have something to get done, do it right away . . . you will feel much happier.

SUPER Words and Promises for a SUPER You!

Little guys can do big things too!

Don't wait— or you'll be late. Do it now!

Make work FUN and it won't be so hard!

Questions to Talk about with Your SUPER Mom and Dad

What are some things you can do around the house to be more helpful?

Why is hard work better than laziness?

A Prayer

God, help me to get my chores done and do the right thing always.
Amen

God thinks YOU are SUPER and wants you to . . .

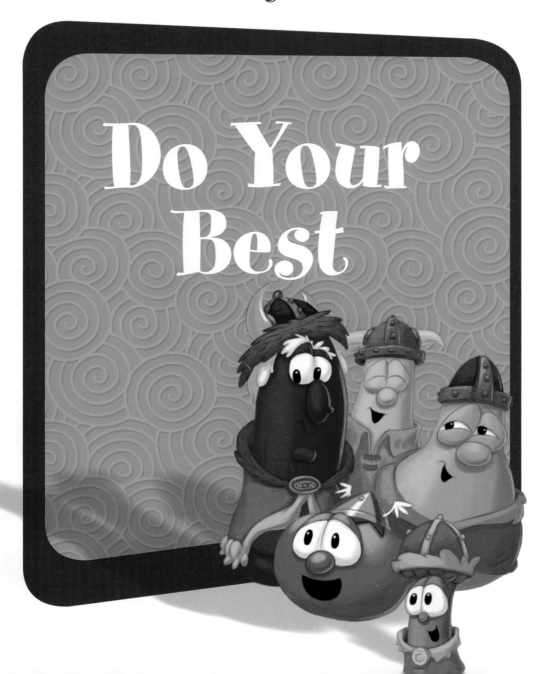

Do Your Best

The Halfhearted Viking

Even Vikings need a vacation. And one of the favorite Viking vacation spots was the Pillage Inn Resort on the coast of Denmark.

"Say cheese!" Sven shouted, snapping a group photo by the pool. A huge sign greeted them that read "Have a Plunderful Time at the Pillage Inn."

It was as perfect as a postcard—until the monster showed up.

203

Well, actually, things started going wrong even before the monster came along. It all went downhill the moment the Vikings met the hotel owner, Halfdanish, and his little dog, Beo-Woof.

Halfdanish was a Viking, too, but he was a halfhearted Viking. He never put his whole heart into anything. He never did his best, especially when it came to running the hotel.

Halfdanish carried their suitcases only halfway to their rooms and then dropped them on the floor. "It's the best I can do," he said.

Even more shocking, the hotel room was half the size of a normal room, and the beds were half the size of normal beds.

"I thought we were getting king-sized beds," said Olaf.

"Sorry. We only have peasant-sized beds," said Halfdanish. "It's the best I can do."

Every day, the maids cleaned only half of the room.

The restaurant served half-cooked meals. And the waiters spilled half of the food on the Vikings.

The vikings tried their best to enjoy themselves anyway. During their first hour at the Pillage Inn, Sven had already taken 1,214 photos.

But when Ottar and Sven found out that their hotel towels were only half dry, it was time to complain. They went straight to the front desk.

"In addition to the half-dry towels, the TV in our room only shows half of a picture," griped Ottar.

"Sorry, it's the best I can do," Halfdanish said. He shrugged and went back to reading the newspaper.

"Is this really the best you can do?" asked Ottar. "God asks us to serve others with *all* of our heart. When you put all of your heart into something and do your best, it shows that you care. But you don't care about anyone but yourself!"

Halfdanish looked up from his paper and said, "Sorry. What was that you said? I was only half listening."

Ottar let out a groan.

Here's the deal," added Halfdanish, setting down the paper. "I'll give you guys bigger rooms if you do a little something for me."

"What little something?" Ottar asked. He didn't like the sound of this.

"Just get rid of a little pest in our hotel," said Halfdanish.

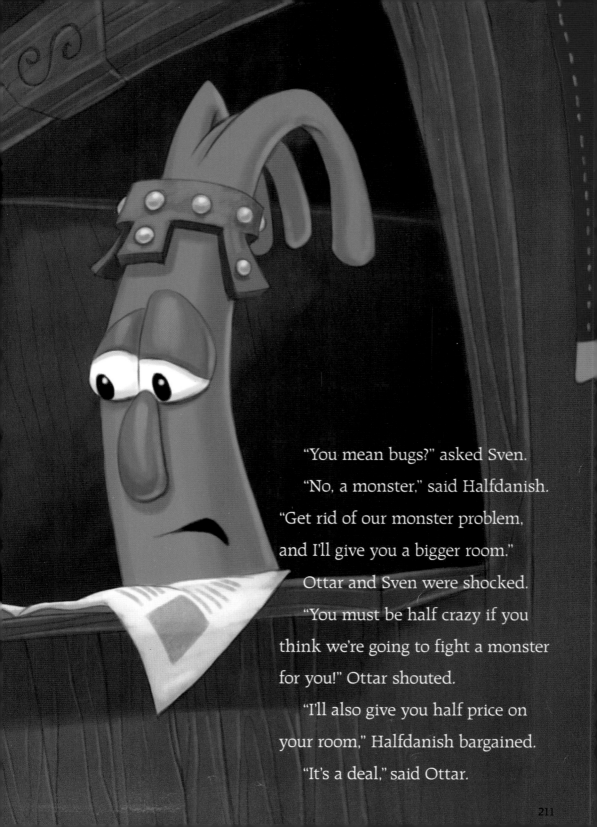

"You mean bugs?" asked Sven.

"No, a monster," said Halfdanish. "Get rid of our monster problem, and I'll give you a bigger room."

Ottar and Sven were shocked.

"You must be half crazy if you think we're going to fight a monster for you!" Ottar shouted.

"I'll also give you half price on your room," Halfdanish bargained.

"It's a deal," said Ottar.

So that very night, Ottar and Sven hid in the storage room next to the kitchen.

"Halfdanish said the monster broke into the hotel last night and took lots of hotel towels," Ottar told Sven.

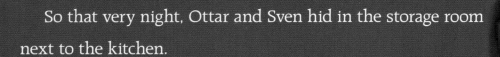

"The horror!" Sven exclaimed. "What kind of beast are we dealing with? What kind of monster would take a hotel towel? What kind of—"

"Sshhhhhh," cried Ottar. "Did you hear that?"

"You mean the sound of me talking?" whispered Sven. "When I talk, I always hear myself. That's the way it usually works."

"No. *That*," said Ottar.

There it was—the sound of a door creaking open. Something had entered the kitchen—something breathing very, very hard.

Ottar peeked through the door.
The shadow of a hideous beast was cast
against the kitchen wall. The monster had
huge spiky horns and a long pointy tail!

"Are you ready?" whispered Ottar.

"Ready," said Sven, trembling.

"Now!" Ottar said.

The two brave Vikings barged into the kitchen.

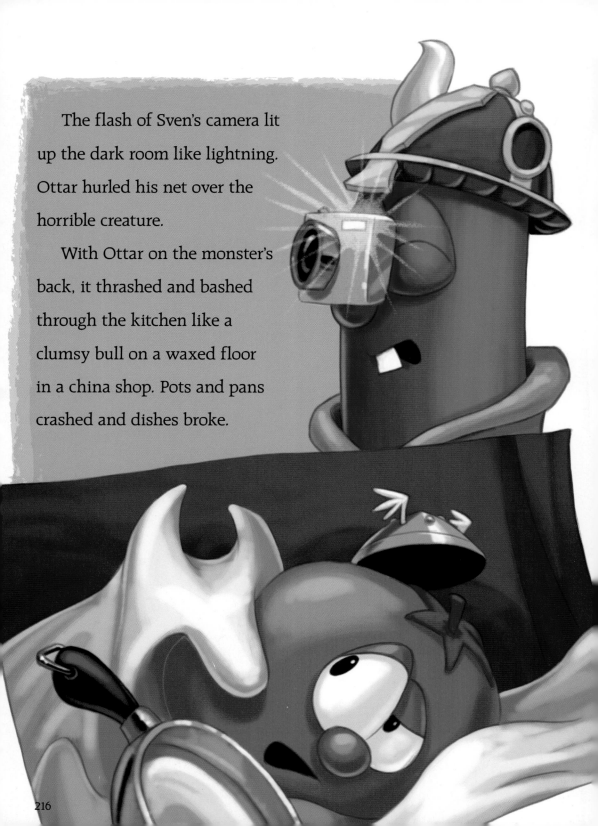

The flash of Sven's camera lit up the dark room like lightning. Ottar hurled his net over the horrible creature.

With Ottar on the monster's back, it thrashed and bashed through the kitchen like a clumsy bull on a waxed floor in a china shop. Pots and pans crashed and dishes broke.

Finally, the creature tumbled to the floor, wrapped up in the net.

CLICK!

Someone turned on the light in the kitchen.

It was Halfdanish, still in his pajamas.

"I was half asleep when I heard the ruckus," said Halfdanish. "Did you capture the monster?"

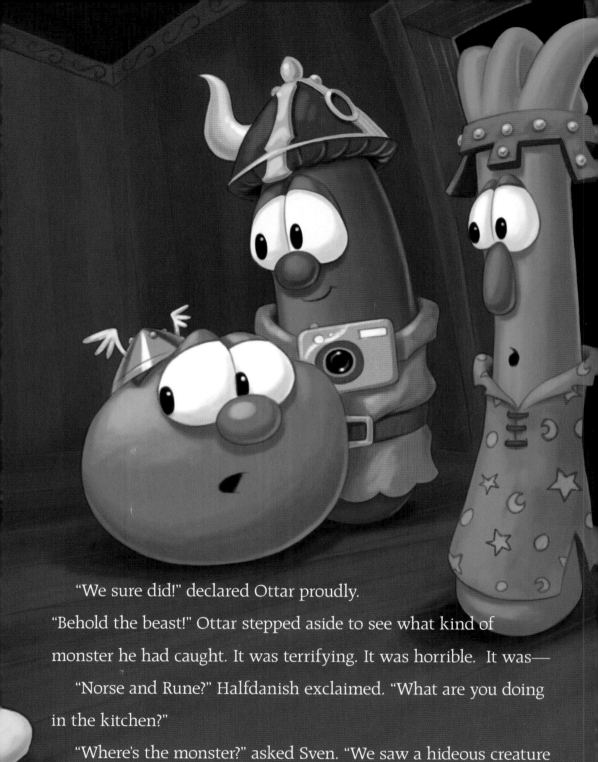

"We sure did!" declared Ottar proudly.

"Behold the beast!" Ottar stepped aside to see what kind of monster he had caught. It was terrifying. It was horrible. It was—

"Norse and Rune?" Halfdanish exclaimed. "What are you doing in the kitchen?"

"Where's the monster?" asked Sven. "We saw a hideous creature with horns and a spiked tail!"

219

"Don't you see, Sven," said Ottar. "They *are* the monster! And look, they're stealing towels again."

"You're fired!" shouted Halfdanish.

"No, wait!" Ottar said. "Maybe they're *not* stealing the towels. I think they're bringing them back. And look, these towels are fluffy clean!"

"Oooooo—lemony fresh!" said Sven, burying his nose in a towel.

"Your employees really care," came a voice from the door. It was the guy from the all-night laundry place. "Norse and Rune weren't happy with half-dry towels in this hotel. So they've been bringing them to me in the middle of the night."

Halfdanish was stunned. "I didn't know how much you cared about this hotel," he said to his two employees.

"They care and do their very best. They're no monster," said the laundry guy.

And that's when it happened. Some how, some way, Halfdanish's heart became whole that night. Norse and Rune had shown him how wonderful it was to put your whole heart into something.

From that moment on, things changed at the Pillage Inn.
Halfdanish made sure the meals were fully cooked, the beds were
fully made, and room service employees brought meals all the way
to the room.

But best of all, Halfdanish found out that doing his best made
him not half happy—but totally happy.

And that isn't half bad.

DEAr AUNT HILDE,
HAVING A PLUNDErFUL TiME iN DeNMARK.
WiSH you were here. WiTh All My heArT,   -SVEN

Work at everything you do with all your heart.
Work as if you were working for the Lord,
not for human masters.

Colossians 3:23

THINK ABOUT THIS...

Sometimes we don't try very hard. But, we are happy when we do our best.

When we don't do our best, it can make you feel bad. So, do your best, even when it is hard. It will make you happier. It will help you to grow up and be very good at what you want to do.

Doing your best can be a lot of fun.

SUPER Words and Promises for a SUPER You!

God made you special so you can do super special things!

Sometimes we don't do our best. Don't give up. You can try to do better next time.

God's way is the best way!

Questions to Talk about with Your SUPER Mom and Dad

How does it make you feel when you do your best?

What is something you want to do better at home? at school? at church?

A Prayer
God, help me do my best today and every day!
Amen

God thinks YOU are SUPER
and wants you to . . .

Be Loving Toward Others

The Surprising Knight

The castle buzzed with excitement and music. **"Ba-ba-ba! Bar-barian!"** sang a strolling pea with a mandolin. "You got me rocking and a rolling, baking and a cooking, Rhubarbarian!"

"I just love that serf music!" the Duke of Scone exclaimed.

"Me too," said Petunia, a Rhubarbarian princess.

Duke and Petunia had their eyes on the prize—and on the pies. They wanted to win the prize for the best pie in the kingdom. In fact, *everyone* wanted to win the Pie Prize, which was going to be given out at the Pie-Palooza Festival.

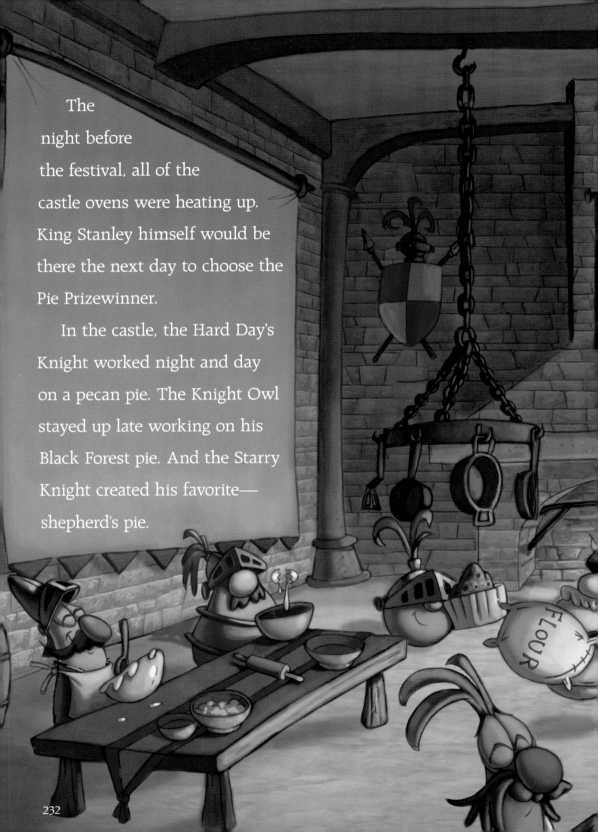

The
night before
the festival, all of the
castle ovens were heating up.
King Stanley himself would be
there the next day to choose the
Pie Prizewinner.

In the castle, the Hard Day's
Knight worked night and day
on a pecan pie. The Knight Owl
stayed up late working on his
Black Forest pie. And the Starry
Knight created his favorite—
shepherd's pie.

As for Duke and Petunia . . . BONK!

"Oops. My mistake," said Duke. He and Petunia had clunked

heads while bending down to pick up their apple pie.

"No, my mistake. You first," Petunia said.

"No, you first," said Duke.

CLUNK!

They both went first and bonked

heads for what had to be the

fourteenth time that day.

BAM! BAM! BAM!

Very confused, Duke glanced at Petunia and asked, "Was that the sound of us clunking heads three more times?"

"No, I think it's the sound of someone knocking on the castle door," Petunia said, with a giggle.

Duke and Petunia looked down from the tower window. An old, old man banged on the door with his walking stick.

But none of the knights on the first floor
would answer the door. They were too busy
baking pies.

"Bah!" scoffed the Knight
Watchman. "It's just an old
man. I'm not letting
him in."

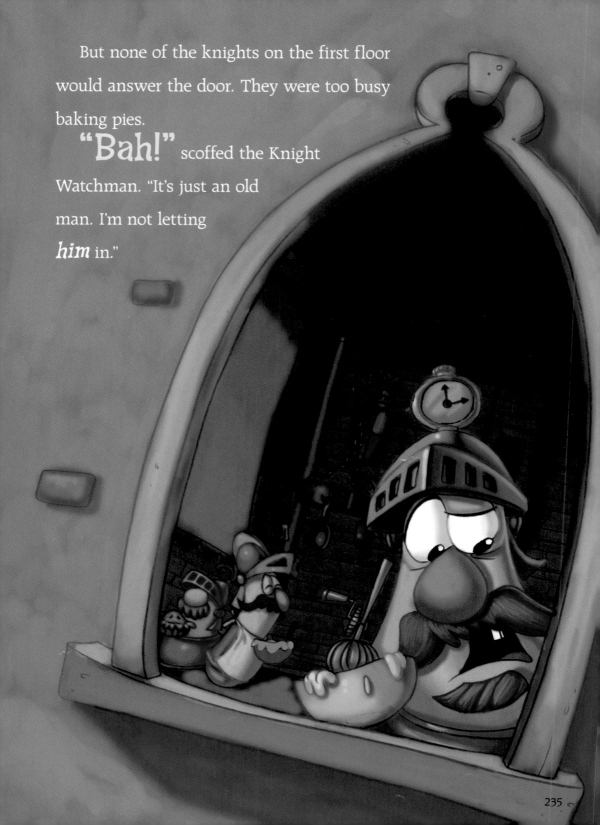

BAM! BAM! BAM!

"How can they leave an old man out in the cold like that?" wondered Duke.

So Duke and Petunia scurried downstairs and pushed open the heavy wooden door.

236

BONK!

Duke and Petunia clunked heads bowing to the old man.

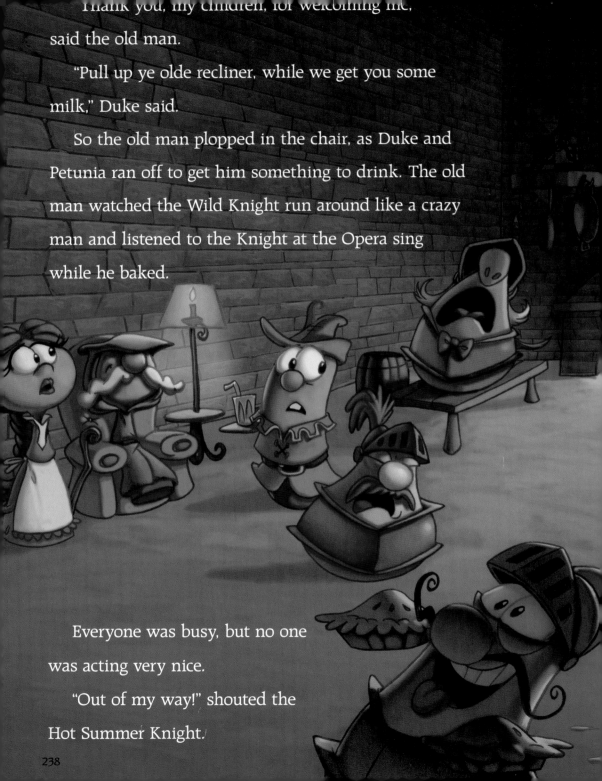

Thank you, my children, for welcoming me,
said the old man.

"Pull up ye olde recliner, while we get you some
milk," Duke said.

So the old man plopped in the chair, as Duke and
Petunia ran off to get him something to drink. The old
man watched the Wild Knight run around like a crazy
man and listened to the Knight at the Opera sing
while he baked.

Everyone was busy, but no one
was acting very nice.

"Out of my way!" shouted the
Hot Summer Knight.

"Work faster!" the Knight Before Last yelled at his assistant, Holly Berry.

Suddenly the Stormy Knight stormed into the dining room, throwing the door open without even looking. The door slammed into the Knight Watchman, knocking his pie right into his face.

SPLAT!

The Knight Watchman was furious! In fact, he was so angry that he pushed over the huge table loaded with pies.

This made *everyone* angry! Furious, all of the knights hurled pies at each other right and left.

SPLAT!

SPLAT!

SPLAT!

The Knight at the Opera tried to calm
everyone with a little knight music. "I wish they
all could be Rhubarbarian girls!" he sang. "Well,
East Coast pies are—"

SPLAT!
(It's hard to sing with
pie in your face.)

Pies were flying so wildly that one of them even smacked the old man square in the kisser.

SPLAT!

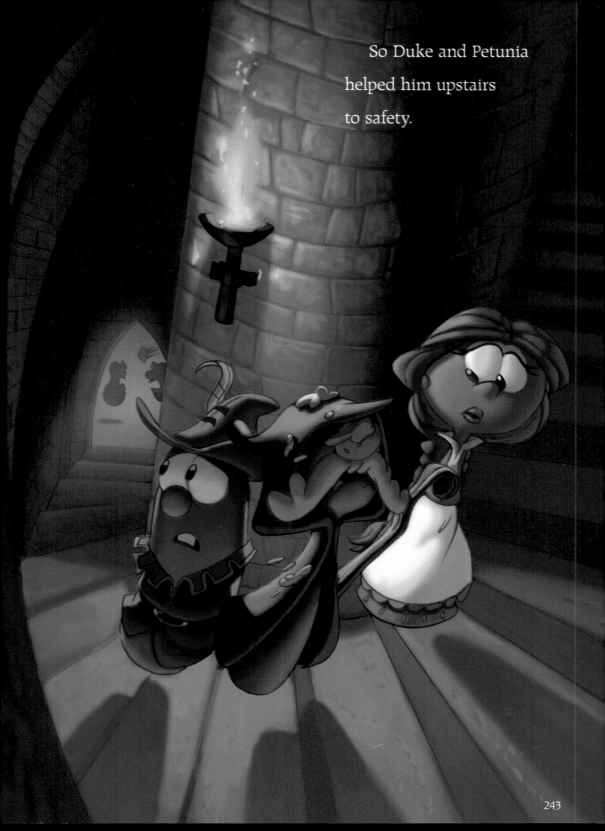

So Duke and Petunia
helped him upstairs
to safety.

243

CLUNK! Duke and Petunia bonked heads as they both bent down to wipe pie from the old man's face.

"I can't believe they did this to you," said Petunia. "How can we make it up to you?"

The old man eyed the apple pie that Duke and Petunia had baked. "Well—I am a bit hungry," the old man said.

CLUNK!

Duke and Petunia looked at each other. They had spent all
day baking that pie for the contest! But they knew that God
would rather they feed a hungry man than win a silly prize.
"Dig in!" Duke shouted.

By morning, the entire castle was a mess. It had been a frightful night of fighting.

Suddenly the Knight Watchman shouted, "The king is coming!" Sure enough, a royal carriage was winding its way toward the castle. The knights hurried to clean up the mess, but it was too little—too late.

All of the knights lined up in front of the castle as the king's carriage came to a stop. The door swung open and out stepped . . .

. . . a pea?!?

"*Bonjour!*" shouted the king's helper, a pea named Jean-Claude.

"But where's King Stanley?" the Winter's Knight asked.

"Right behind you!" shouted a voice from the castle.

The knights spun around and nearly fainted. The old man, standing in the castle door, yanked off his hood. It was King Stanley!

"But . . . but . . ." The knights did not know what to say.

"When you became knights, you promised to obey the most important rule in our kingdom: to love God and love each other," King Stanley said. "I wanted to find out if you really put your words into action."

To see if the knights would act lovingly, King Stanley had disguised himself as an old man and arrived a night early. Unfortunately, the knights had not lived up to their promise.

249

It was certainly a time for surprises. But the biggest surprise was what happened next.

King Stanley held up an empty pie pan for all to see. "**_This_** is the prizewinning pie!" King Stanley announced. "And the winners are Duke and Petunia!"

"But there's nothing in the pan," pointed out the Scary Knight.

"There's nothing in the pan because they shared this pie lovingly," said King Stanley. "That makes it the greatest pie of all!"

Now, Duke and Petunia did not win because their pie tasted the best or looked the best. They won because they showed their love for others. They won because they treated others like kings.

So King Stanley handed Duke and Petunia the Pie Prize, and they bowed to the crowd. CLUNK!

It was one of those days.

CLUNK!

Dear children, don't just talk about love.
Put your love into action. Then it will truly be love.

1 John 3:18

THINK ABOUT THIS...

When we fight and are mean to each other none of us are very happy. It makes it hard to smile and feel good. God wants us to be happy, so He tells us to love each other. God even wants us to love people that aren't super nice.

Your parents and teachers tell you to love others and be kind. That's because they want what is best for you. They want you to be happy on the inside. Make today—and tomorrow—very special. Love everybody you see.

SUPER Words and Promises for a SUPER You!

It makes God very happy when we show love to others.

When you make others happy, you become happier too.

Today is a good day to be kind!

254

Questions to Talk about with Your SUPER Mom and Dad

What are ways you can show people you love them?

How about your friends? How about your parents?

How about your brother or sister?

How does it make you feel when you know someone loves you very much?

A Prayer

Dear Lord, help me make Your world a better place by sharing my things and being loving toward others. Amen

The Good, The Bad, and The Silly
Story by: Doug Peterson
Illustrated by: Tom Bancroft and Rob Corley
Colored by: Jon Conkling

The Kid Crayon Caper
Story by: Bobbi JG Weiss & David Cody Weiss
Illustrated by: Greg Hardin and John Trent

The Fastest Dodge Ball in the West
Story by: Doug Peterson
Illustrated by: Tom Bancroft and Rob Corley
Colored by: Jon Conkling

The Chicken Noodle Super Bowl
Story by: Doug Peterson
Illustrated by: Michael Moore

Giddy Up and Wait
Story by: Tracey West
Illustrated by: Tom Bancroft and Rob Corley
Colored by: Jon Conkling

Who's Afraid of the Big Bad Mop?
Story by: Doug Peterson
Illustrated by: Greg Hardin and John Trent

LarryBoy versus Spud the Dud
Story by: Doug Peterson
Illustrated by: Tom Bancroft and Rob Corley
Colored by: Jon Conkling

The Halfhearted Viking
Story by: Doug Peterson
Illustrated by: Warner McGee

The Surprising Knight
Story by: Doug Peterson
Illustrated by: Tod Carter and Joe Spadaford